THE SALAMANDER CHILL

Eric Ward, Newcastle solicitor, was distinctly uneasy on the board of Martin and Channing, merchant bankers, and never more so than now when the bank had been called in by the Salamander Corporation to help fight off a hostile takeover bid. The defensive strategy invol... ...ler chill. ... 4/92 e Salan... ...r who ... ...h the C... ...t that ...; Eric ...s wife'... ...d saw ... ...d towa... ...s invo...

THE SALAMANDER CHILL

Roy Lewis

ATLANTIC LARGE PRINT
Chivers Press, Bath, England.
Curley Publishing, Inc.,
South Yarmouth, Mass., USA.

Library of Congress Cataloging in Publication Data

Lewis, Roy. 1933–
   The salamander chill / Roy Lewis.
     p.   cm.—(Atlantic large print)
   ISBN 1–55504–903–6 (lg. print)
   1. Large type books I. Title.
[PR6062.E954S25 1989]
823′.914—dc19   89–30252
                                          CIP

British Library Cataloguing in Publication Data

Lewis, J. R. (John Royston), *1933*–
   The salamander chill
   I. Title
   823′.914 [F]

   ISBN 0–7451–9504–0
   ISBN 0–7451–9516–4 Pbk

This Large Print edition is published by Chivers Press, England, and Curley Publishing, Inc, U.S.A. 1989

Published in the British Commonwealth by arrangement with William Collins Sons & Co. Ltd and in the U.S.A. with St. Martin's Press

U.K. Hardback ISBN 0 7451 9504 0
U.K. Softback ISBN 0 7451 9516 4
U.S.A. Softback ISBN 1 55504 903 6

4/92 CURLEY 6.95

CHAPTER ONE

1

A heatwave had been idling over the Northumberland hills. It had brought shirtsleeve weather to an area where the inhabitants were more accustomed to treating June with circumspection, going about their business with their coat collars turned up.

Eric Ward had taken a few days' leave from his office at the Quayside in Newcastle. His work in personal terms had slowed somewhat of late, since he had taken on an assistant to deal with the commercial side of the business—an aspect of the practice that had grown on the mercantile side. Young Ted Grainger had proved to be keen, enthusiastic, and well able to cope, as Anne had forcefully reminded Eric when he had doubted whether he could afford to leave the practice for a week or so. 'What the hell else did you take him on for if not to let him get on with the business?' she had demanded. It was not an argument easy to counter.

So he had been able to take advantage of the early summer weather and enjoy long afternoon walks in the meadows and lanes of the estates around Sedleigh Hall. He had been able to afford the luxury of lunch with Anne on the terrace, with its distant view of

Cheviot, blue in the afternoon haze—sole, a chilled glass of Chablis, fresh strawberries—and he had indulged himself further with an occasional siesta while Anne busied herself on the phone, discussing the management of the Morcomb Estates and their vast holdings.

He even managed to avoid feeling guilty about it. The fact that the office was working without him, and Anne was conducting her own affairs without reference to him, gave no sour chill to the afternoon: he realized he was coming to terms with having a rich wife who could buy and sell a hundred practices like his own. And as for enjoying her house and land, well, he knew deep inside that he was still his own man, he had retained his own independence, and even the glaucoma seemed to have been kept at bay of recent months with the pilocarpine easing the occasional discomfort.

The afternoon had stretched out like a sleeping cat and the shadows had begun to lengthen before Anne returned to the terrace, glass of wine in her hand. She moved her chair to take advantage of the dying sun, leaned over Eric and kissed him, lingeringly, on the mouth. When she moved away, to sit down, he smiled. 'You're pleased with yourself.'

'I am.'

'Want to tell me?'

'No.' She grinned wickedly, sipped her

wine, hugged the secret of her pleasure to herself. Eric smiled. She would tell him in due course, but right now she wanted to savour her triumph, gloat over it with an almost childish pleasure, and when that was sated there would be time to tell her husband, and experience the whole thing again, through his eyes. Eric put his head back, enjoying the quiet of the hills and the lazy, late afternoon. Soon the dusk would come, softly, bringing with it the crushed-clove smell of night-scented stocks. The swifts would wheel in above their heads in the afterglow. Newcastle would be a world away, the noisy bustling streets, busy in spite of the depression brought about by closure of steel, coal and shipbuilding industries, distant. He could indulge his senses, allow himself the savouring of languid pleasures, like the tasting of a ripe peach.

*　　　*　　　*

'Well, aren't you going to get ready?'

Eric came up muzzily from his doze, focused with difficulty. Anne was leaning towards him, her hair glowing against the dipping sun.

'Ready? For what?'

'Dinner. We have guests.'

'We do?' Eric frowned, clearing his head. 'I don't remember—'

3

'Because I didn't tell you.'

She grabbed his hand, dragged him from his chair and stood close to him, arms wrapped tightly about him. A mischievous light danced in her eyes.

'Your long phone call,' he said, understanding.

'Correct.'

'So someone's coming to dinner.'

'Perspicacious.'

'But you won't tell me who.'

'Of course I will. You only have to ask.'

He tightened his own grip of her body, and the breath whoofed out of her. 'So I'm asking.'

'Well, do it more delicately,' she complained, laughing and struggling against him. 'Now you've asked, I'll tell you. It's Jim Edmonds.'

Eric stared at her, amused. 'That's pretty anti-climactic, for great news. Who the hell is Jim Edmonds?'

'An accountant.'

Eric groaned. 'For dinner? I mean, hell, accountants are more boring even than lawyers!'

'That's a matter of opinion. Besides, he's more of a financial adviser than an accountant.'

'You've *got* financial advisers.'

'And now I've got a new one.'

'You're going to employ him *and* give him

dinner? What exactly does this character Edmonds have, for God's sake?'

She chuckled. 'Information. And from what he told me over the phone, it's the kind of information I've been hoping for.'

'And what kind is that?'

Anne drew away from him and took a look at the bottle of Chablis. There was a little remaining: she glanced at Eric, he shook his head, and she poured what was left in the bottle into her glass. She raised it to him and sipped; she looked very young and very confident and quite beautiful. 'You know I've been advised that the Morcomb holdings aren't spread too wisely at the moment, in view of movements in the marketplace.'

'So you told me.'

'I had a long chat with the accountants some months ago and they came up with a few ideas, but it seemed to me they were just messing about at the edges. You know, not doing anything really *constructive*.'

'They'll hardly be the most entrepreneurial people you'll come across. They'll be protecting your money and their backs.'

Anne nodded. 'I understand that. But to be fair, they made some suggestions when I told them what I had in mind, and the clearest suggestion was that if I was serious, I ought to get a specialist in to advise me.'

'A specialist?'

'In acquisitions.'

'Ahhh . . .' Eric nodded, moving away to the end of the terrace. The hills were darkening now and soon the flight of owls would begin, sailing majestically through the still summer air, predators seeking a swift kill, a gain in the darkness. 'Acquisitions. Yes. A specialism indeed. This is where your Mr Edmonds comes in?'

'That's right. He's the guy they all seem to recommend as the bright, up-and-coming star in the field. Apparently, he worked for one of the big accounting firms and very quickly got into the business of acquisitions. Proved himself to be good at it. Moved a couple of times, always into bigger operations. Then set out on his own, freelancing, contracting his services where they were best paid. He's been in the States for some time, doing some searches there for several clients. I was lucky to get hold of him.'

'Hence the triumph.'

Anne ducked her head. 'Sorry about that. But it wasn't just *getting* him. I gave him a contract some ten weeks ago. No, it's the fact that he's done his acquisitions search and it sounds as if he's come up with something interesting that'll fit our particular bill very well.'

'*Our* bill?'

'Darling, you know all that's mine is yours, except my bathroom, which is where I'm headed now while you clutter up your own.

6

He'll be here at seven-thirty, driving up from Newcastle, and he's bringing his fiancée with him. She's called Karen O'Neill. A fashion model, I understand. And from what he says, quite stunning.' The mischief was back in her eyes. 'He's quite young, too.' She finished her drink hastily at the look in his eyes and stood up. 'Now if you're going to look like that you can share my shower: it might help you to cool off.'

In practice, quite the reverse, Eric considered, and decided to take up the offer.

*   *   *

They were both downstairs by seven-fifteen, Anne elegant in a cool blue dress that complemented her eyes beautifully, and while she took a pre-dinner gin and tonic Eric settled for a glass of mineral water. Alcohol could be taken in moderation, his doctors had advised him, but Eric seemed to have lost his taste for whisky and now drank only wine and, rarely, brandy.

By eight o'clock Jim Edmonds had not arrived. Eric wandered across to the window. 'You think he's playing hard to get?'

As though in answer he caught the flash of headlights on the hill: a car, making its way over the brow, dipping down into the hollow and the entrance to the Sedleigh Hall driveway. Anne was at Eric's side. 'I expect that's him.' She sounded slightly nettled. Mr Edmonds might be a successful acquisitions expert but he seemed less adept at acquiring a reputation for good manners.

A few minutes later, he was announced.

As Anne walked forward, extending her hand, Edmonds was already apologizing. She shook her head, coolly, and looked behind him: he was alone.

'That's the reason why I'm so late,' he explained, ducking his head in embarrassment. 'Karen . . . she phoned from London. I'd gone to meet the train, you see, and she wasn't on it, and so I went back to the flat and then she rang . . . she couldn't make it. I . . . I guess I should have rung Sedleigh Hall then, to warn you, but, well . . . I was a bit put out, you know, and not thinking straight . . .'

'Think no more of it,' Anne said quietly. 'This is my husband, Eric.'

'I've heaard about you,' Edmonds said, gripping Eric's hand with a fierce nervousness. 'You have a practice down at the Quayside, I believe.'

'I'm never quite certain whether it's flattering to be known about by accountants.' He caught Anne's warning glance and smiled, decided to be on his best behaviour. 'Would you care for a drink?'

'If it's not too late,' Edmonds said awkwardly. 'I mean, if dinner—'

'Dinner can wait,' Anne said crisply.

'A whisky, then, please.'

Eric poured him a generous tot, added water at Edmonds's request and then stood back. A clumsy young man, he thought, with the kind of clumsiness a woman would find endearing and a man irritating. He was big, well over six feet, with broad shoulders that seemed to strain at the oatmeal-coloured lightweight suit he wore. He had a long face, well chiselled features somewhat marred by a heavy chin, and a wispy moustache that somehow emphasized a social immaturity. His movements were heavy, he seemed to lurch rather than walk, and as a child, Eric considered, he might have had a reputation for breaking things. But never intentionally, never that. Maybe that was why Eric disliked him, because of his clumsiness.

Or maybe because he was little older than Anne.

'Karen's very busy, you see,' Edmonds was explaining earnestly. 'She's contracted to a fashion agency which works her pretty hard. Don't get me wrong, there's plenty of money in the fashion modelling business, but it has to be earned. Hot lights, long hours. That's what she says.'

'And fame,' Eric suggested.

'Yes, that too. But she'll give it up when we marry.'

Anne laughed. 'That sounds like a typical

northern male attitude!'

'No, we've agreed on it,' Edmonds hurried to say, but something in his tone made Eric believe the agreement was hardly finalized. 'My job, you see, it means necessarily I have to travel a lot, and it just wouldn't make sense her being in one part of the world and me in another.' His eyes were angry suddenly, hints of a smouldering dispute smoking deep inside him.

He finished his drink in a long swallow: Eric offered him another and Edmonds took it. The fact that Karen O'Neill was not with him was clearly a matter of some importance: he was bothered by it, possibly because he regarded his meeting with Anne here at Sedleigh Hall as of some consequence to him, an occasion that should have rightly demanded the support of his fiancée. Or maybe it was something else, something darker and deeper in the relationship that was bothering him. It was none of Eric's business. He handed the drink to Edmonds. The man's hands were large and powerful, backed by fair hair as blond as the thick, stiff hair of his head. They did not look like an accountant's hands. They seemed to lack . . . precision, and neatness.

But this man wasn't an accountant. He was an acquisitions expert. And acquisitions could be brutal.

'Shall we go in to dinner?' Anne suggested.

10

'Please, bring your drink with you.'

Edmonds didn't. He gulped it down. There was a rather good Fleurie with dinner tonight and a cool Sancerre with the fish. Eric guessed they might have to offer the impetuous Mr Edmonds a bed for the night rather than have him brave the Northumberland police patrols in a state of inebriation.

Over dinner, Edmonds did enjoy both the Sancerre and the Fleurie, but carefully, and with an air of quiet appreciation that did something to soften Eric's first impressions of the man. One impression that did not change however was that of Edmonds's obsession with his fiancée: he talked constantly of her over dinner, explaining about the contracts she had undertaken, Givenchy, *Vanity Fair*, Chagrin. Once or twice Eric caught Anne's glance and raised one eyebrow and she gave him a little impatient shake of the head. She was too good a hostess to force Edmonds towards the business in hand, but over coffee the man seemed at last to unwind and relate more sensibly to his surroundings, to the fact that Karen O'Neill was not with him, and that Anne Ward had other things than fashion modelling to discuss.

'I'm afraid I've been boring you,' he suggested.

'Not at all. It's been . . . interesting. I must admit I can't remember having seen

11

Karen's name . . .'

'Modelling can be a bit anonymous. The face, but not the name, that sort of thing. However, I'm aware I've trespassed on your time and your hospitality overlong before coming to the reason why I'm really here. As I told you over the phone, I think I've found what you want.'

Anne stopped him, raising a warning hand. She smiled. 'I think I should explain, my husband and I have business interests which rarely overlap. He plays little or no part in the management of Morcomb Estates; consequently, I haven't told him just what arrangement you and I have come to, Mr Edmonds. I wonder whether you'd mind filling him in on the background?'

Edmonds nodded and turned to glance towards Eric. 'How much do you know about the acquisitions business, Mr Ward?'

'Treat me as a tyro,' Eric replied, studiously avoiding Anne's glance.

Jim Edmonds furrowed his brow and nodded. 'Okay. But I guess you'll already be aware of my credentials and track record . . . Mrs Ward will have told you? In brief, a few leading accountancy firms, striking out on a freelance basis, a couple of big American contracts and a lot of luck—'

'And now a certain reputation of success,' Anne intervened, making the point to Eric.

'Okay. Well, I'll tell it like I told it to Mrs

12

Ward at the beginning. It's the takeover bids for large companies that make the news but the vast majority of acquisitions are of unquoted companies, or divisions and subsidiaries of quoted ones. But before anyone starts putting his foot into this kind of pool it's necessary to determine the reasons for doing so. You may want to acquire a business because of its entrepreneurial management; you may want to pump some financial injections into an ailing company to turn it around and make a fast few bucks.'

'Or even pounds,' Eric said.

'Sorry, a couple of months in the States . . . Anyway, I talked things through with Mrs Ward and was satisfied that she was thinking of acquisitions for the right reasons. She was looking to diversify the holdings, invest surplus funds from existing operations, and needed my advice to determine if the commercial rationale was sound. Then, we agreed, I should be put under contract to discover what relevant opportunities might exist out there in the market place.'

'We even got into a discussion of synergy,' Ann said, making a little *moue* in Eric's direction.

'And what might that be?'

Edmonds shrugged. 'I think your wife's playing a game with you, Mr Ward. Synergy can be described as a case of $2 + 2 = 5$. For example, if you can integrate and rationalize

13

the sales forces of two companies following an acquisition you *might* achieve the benefits of synergy. On the other hand, you might think you've achieved the benefits but overlook the initial expense and delay in setting the whole thing up. There are hidden costs: you have to take them into account. Buying a company at a bargain price can be superficially attractive. But it's best to step warily.'

Eric was not certain why he had been drawn into this game of Anne's; he carefully kept his distance from Morcomb Estates matters, even though he *had* been drawn in, unwillingly, once or twice. Even so, he now began to get interested in spite of himself. 'So what exactly have you been doing for Morcomb Estates?' he asked.

'The first step was to define an acquisition profile. It was all a bit delayed, because I've had a long job in the States I had to complete before I could spend too much time for Morcomb, but the general idea is to determine just what kind of business is best going to suit Morcomb holdings and future strategy.'

'We talked about things like the market segments I should be thinking about,' Anne added. 'How much cash I was likely to have available for purchase, what might be the minimum size of company we should go for—'

'A most important point,' Edmonds

14

interrupted, warming now as he talked of things in which he was professionally expert. 'You see, many unquoted companies start as family affairs and end up too overly dependent upon one man or a small group of people. Now the question is, should you buy into such a company? It could represent a high degree of vulnerability to the guy making the acquisition, believe me—at least, until he can arrange for some kind of experienced management support. That can take a lot of time and money—and it won't be included in the purchase price! Then, there's the further question of profitability. Unless you intend treating the acquisition as a tax device—'

'Which I do not,' Anne added. 'I want a working investment.'

'—then you have to look to something which is going to present at least a tolerable level of profitability. Ideally, it should already exist in the company you go for; you should certainly have a pretty good idea of what needs to be done to achieve it if it isn't there.'

'I imagine you'll also want to consider things like management style if you're going to retain existing personnel,' Eric suggested.

'Very much so.' Edmonds cocked a quizzical eyebrow. 'I'm not making this too obvious for you?'

'I told you. Teach me.' Even if I don't know why, but can guess, Eric thought.

'Okay, well, there's no such thing as the perfect company for acquisition purposes,' Edmonds continued, 'but we can have a good shot at picking the winners.'

'How?'

'Desk research mainly,' Edmonds replied with a disarming frankness. 'You've got to know where to look, of course, but most of the research can be done by reading company reports, the Extel cards, financial surveys published on business sectors, and there are a number of on-line electronic database services now available that'll give you unquoted company information.'

'And you've now completed all that,' Eric said.

'And come up with a suggestion,' Anne added.

'That's about the size of it, Mrs Ward. And I think the suggestion is a sound one.'

'The name of the company?'

'Roger Graham, Ltd.'

*　　*　　*

As Eric had guessed might be the case, they had to offer Edmonds a room for the night. As he warmed to the discussion, so he warmed to the cognac Anne supplied and he was certainly in no fit state to make the long drive back to Newcastle that night. Even so, there was something nervous about the way

16

he attacked the bottle. Eric commented upon it as he and Anne prepared for bed.

'Drowning devils,' he suggested.

'What?'

'That young man . . . the way he was drinking later on this evening, I got the impression he was trying to kill off something unpleasant. He's got something on his mind apart from business.'

'It's obvious,' Anne agreed. 'Karen O'Neill. She let him down badly, I think, as far as he's concerned. I mean, it makes no difference to me, she was just going to be a social passenger—'

'Like me.'

Anne ignored the remark. 'But he clearly felt that she should have made an effort to be here this evening and consequently he feels let down—and the whole thing's preying on his mind.'

'Maybe a culmination of events.'

'Incompatible careers.'

'Something like that. So aren't you glad we go our separate ways?' Eric tested her.

Anne slipped into bed and sat up, staring at him. Her shoulders glowed in the subdued light and she looked very warm and desirable. A bad time to be talking business: he could be malleable on such occasions.

'Eric . . .'

'Don't tell me. I wasn't there just as a social passenger.'

17

'I need your help.'

'Why? Morcomb Estates run very efficiently while I'm well away from the whole thing. You're more than able; you know what you want for the companies; you've got independent legal and financial advice. What would you want from me?'

'You're a *man*, Eric.'

'I know. I proved it in the shower, earlier.'

'Be serious. You know what I mean.'

He knew what she was driving at. He recalled the conversation with Jim Edmonds earlier that evening.

★   ★   ★

'In looking around at the acquisitions possibilities,' Edmonds had said, 'I finally came to the conclusion that as far as Morcomb Estates was concerned the best bet would be to concentrate on the more attractive, rapidly growing market segments. In recent years a number of unquoted companies have developed micro-processor-based energy management systems for buildings. Now this is a market with a huge potential, but it does require a substantial amount of investment in research and development.'

'Surely an area for large company support?' Eric queried.

'That's so. It's why some big companies

18

have bought into unquoted companies in this sector, because it's pretty difficult to pull together an experienced team on the R and D side. Otherwise, there's lengthy development time facing you.'

'And Roger Graham, Ltd?'

'Have lost their way. There are two operations involved,' Edmonds explained earnestly. 'They've done a great deal of research work on energy management but their original base was in the graphic arts. The old man, Roger Graham himself, started the whole thing some forty years ago and built up a sound graphics business on Tyneside. His elder son, Nick, kicked against his father's traces early on and went to University to read maths—but then got hooked on computing. Two years after university he came into his father's business after all because he'd seen the potential of the computer in the field of graphics. Roger Graham was no fool: he saw the chances that lay ahead. Now, they've been running for some years a small but successful business making computerized equipment for the graphic arts industry.'

'So how have they lost their way?'

Jim Edmonds. pulled a wry face and shrugged. 'It's the old story, I suppose. I told you the old patriarch was cunning enough to see the potential in Nick's ideas for change. But it's another story if young Nick comes up

19

with another idea, which will demand significant investment, and the old man can still see legs in the original company. *Particularly* if the new idea moves away from the field of graphics entirely.'

'There's conflict between father and son?'

'You could certainly say that.'

Eric looked across to Anne, who had been sitting silently. Her features were passive; clearly, there was yet more to come.

'I wouldn't have thought,' Eric said slowly, 'that a company riven apart in this way would make a good investment potential.'

'Depends on the circumstances,' Edmonds replied, scratching his chin in a nervous, jerky gesture. 'The conflict doesn't end with Roger and Nick Graham. There's another son: Chris. The younger brother always has it tough, I think, if his sibling is overly successful, or has a dominating personality. That's the situation with Nick and Chris Graham. There's a resentment there, which takes the effect of Chris wanting anything his brother doesn't. And most of all, Chris wants to get out of his brother's shadow.'

'What's that mean in practical terms?'

'Roger Graham wants to build on the computerized graphics business, and resists the investment required by Nick to expand into energy management. Nick is fighting his father, and is confident he's right—moreover, he has most of the staff with him, even though they have no final say, of course, in any decisions. It's a three shareholding situation.'

'And Chris Graham?'

Edmonds blinked. 'He just wants out.'

'A plague on both their houses, you mean?' Eric asked.

'Precisely. He wants to take what money he can and run. He has no interest in the company, and he certainly does not want to see further investment being ploughed back into expensive new developments.'

'This all sounds to me like a rats' nest,' Eric doubted.

'There's one final point to be made,' Edmonds said, leaning back in his chair and sipping his cognac thoughtfully. 'The old man himself.'

'Yes?'

'Three months ago he suffered a heart attack. He's on the way out. He's still the major shareholder and they need his decision to go any particular way, but he knows his time is limited and he'll want a solution which satisfies two imcompatibles: the safe future of the company he built from nothing, and his dynastic dreams which are foundering on personalities.'

Don't they always, Eric thought to himself. 'You got all this out of company reports?'

Edmonds smiled beneath his wispy moustache. He had good teeth and the smile

21

was engaging. 'There are grapevines,' he said non-committally.

'And you consider Grahams are the stuff of which successful acquisitions are made?' Eric asked.

'In my view they're ripe—and they don't come any riper. Maybe I should sketch out my reasons for the advice I'm giving Mrs Ward and Morcomb Estates. I'm advising the opening of negotiations with Roger Graham, Ltd for these reasons.' He flicked up a finger. 'First, there's the market potential in this particular field.'

'What *is* the potential?'

'Exports have been limited by lack of finance. A capital injection at this stage could give the company access to distribution networks abroad—especially in the States— and to field sales forces that could more than double the company's profitability.'

'Right, that's one reason.'

Edmonds raised a second finger. 'Not to be ignored is the possibility of later sale. If Morcomb Estates went in, did the job right, the company could be sold off at a considerable profit within five years. It just needs help at this moment to get off the plateau.'

'I imagine there might be social implications, also.'

Edmonds paused, looked at Eric in surprise. He nodded. 'Well, yes, of course, causing any company on Tyneside to grow will create employment and that's a considerable benefit to the area.'

'Does that play any part in company thinking?'

'On Roger Graham's part, certainly: he's had some of his work force a long time. Nick . . . he's just for expansion, and thinks only of efficiency. I must say, though, Mr Ward, the social implications rarely figure largely in the acquiring company's calculations.'

'Just asking,' Eric said mildly.

'The third consideration,' Edmonds went on, flicking up a third finger, 'is the particular dissension which currently exists in Roger Graham, Ltd. What we have is an almost classic situation: a dispute as to how the company is best managed for the future; a leading personality who is on the verge of retirement; a major shareholder who wishes to expand but cannot take the board with him in his thinking; a major shareholder who is unwilling to provide more equity capital against a background where company borrowings are already at a realistic limit. It all adds up to one common thread that must be already running through their minds even before we make any approach.'

'Selling the company,' Anne intervened quietly, 'and retaining the existing management team, might provide the solution they all require.'

'That's it precisely.' Edmonds nodded. He hesitated, then glanced at Anne and gnawed his lip. 'There is one further issue, however, which I've already mentioned to Mrs Ward. Roger Graham, Ltd is a typical Tyneside firm.'

Eric was not certain what Edmonds meant. He shook his head, frowning. 'You mean they're under financial pressure?'

'No, not that. Roger and Nick Graham, they're carved out of the same basic material. Brought up in the North, fiercely independent, fixed in their views for all their undoubted entrepreneurial skills. And one very firm view they have is that women belong in the kitchen, not the boardroom.'

There was a short silence. Eric smiled. 'It's odd, isn't it—historically, I mean? In reality, the men only *thought* they ruled the roost. While they crowed, the women got on with the business, controlling the money in the family, making everything tick . . .'

'Still a fact, Mr Ward. The Grahams have fixed views. They are not going to like dealing with a woman—'

'They'll be dealing with Morcomb Estates,' Anne insisted.

'Owned—and *run*—by a woman,' Edmonds replied. 'Please, I'm just giving you the facts as I perceive them. What it means is there'll be some very tough bargaining, and the tougher, and more resistant to common logic, because of the attitude. I merely make the point: but Grahams still remain my best choice for an acquisition by Morcomb Estates, and I shall of course be happy to assist in future negotiations in any way you desire . . .'

★   ★   ★

'We could play their game, darling,' Anne said, her fingertips light on his shoulder, gentle, soft. 'I mean, if they think I'm ruled by my big brute of a husband, if they think you're really the driving force behind Morcomb Estates—'

'It won't work, Anne,'

'Why not? It might be rather fun to fool them. I'd quite enjoy sitting there, maybe acting the secretary or something, letting them think my name on the company is just a tax fiddle, a device for getting the Inland Revenue off our backs. They'd think you were ever so clever, doing that—'

'Anne, I tell you it won't work,' Eric said quietly. 'To begin with, it's not what you want. You'd rather muscle it out with them personally, show them what you're made of, and force them to accept you're as good as, or better than, they are.'

She was silent for a little while. 'You're right, of course,' she said at last. 'But on the other hand, it would be even better if we were

25

working *together* on this one. I know I'll have Morcomb advisers, but it's not the same, Eric, as having you there with me, supporting me—'

'You don't *need* my support, and you know it.'

'But if there *was* a need?'

Eric made no reply, but took her fingers and kissed them lightly and then her mouth, more firmly.

Later as he drifted on the edge of sleep he was vaguely aware of Anne's voice, as though at a great distance. 'It's a funny thing, you know . . . in spite of all Jim Edmonds says, I can't say I've ever heard of this famous fashion model fiancée of his. Do you think she really exists, Eric?'

It hardly seemed worth fighting sleep to answer.

2

Two days later the weather changed to a more normal, cool rain, and with it ended Eric's relaxation at Sedleigh Hall. If he were honest with himself, he thought, he would have to admit that he had had enough of the lazy life, and it was time to get back to the office. He drove down to Newcastle on the Wednesday evening and stayed at the flat, then went down to the Quayside and the office next morning.

There were a number of messages waiting

for him; he scanned the list, frowned at one of them and then went through to the office used by Ted Grainger. The young solicitor was at his desk, shirtsleeved, a pile of documents in front of him.

Eric sat down. 'Like your tan,' he said.

'Great weekend. Went sailing off Shields.'

'What's she like?'

'Boat or girl?'

'Both.'

'About equal. Both move like a dream.' Ted Grainger grinned, teeth white against the deep tan of his skin. 'You look pretty healthy yourself. Life of the landed gent and all that. I'm surprised you even bothered coming back.'

'And leave you to bring about the financial collapse of the multi-million pound empire I've constructed here? To hell with that.' Eric grimaced, pointing to the documentation in front of Grainger. 'That business, or just for show, Ted?'

'The show's been on at the Five Bridges Hotel, *Mr* Ward, with some very splendid lunches; *this* is where it all hits the fan: we're being asked to sort out the marine contracts on the Dawson insurance claims.'

'*All* of them?'

'All.'

'So we'll be eating for the next year or so, then.'

'You could say so, boss.' Grainger grinned

27

at him, pleased at Eric's understatement, aware he had pulled off a major coup, getting the Dawson business. And knowing too he was more than pulling his weight in Eric's firm.

'Well, I'd better get on with my own desk-clearing,' Eric said, hauling himself to his feet.

'One thing you'd better respond to, Eric. He's been on the phone. Didn't sound too pleased you'd taken time off.'

Eric thought about the messages on his desk. He could guess which one Grainger was referring to. 'I'm on the phone at Sedleigh Hall. He could have tried me there.'

'So I suggested. I told him you had all mod. cons. in that desirable residence. He went sniffy, said he didn't believe in disturbing a man at home.'

'The hell he doesn't. All right, I'll deal with it. Thanks, Ted.'

Eric wandered back to his office, arranging with his secretary for a cup of coffee on the way, and then sat behind his desk, scanning the messages again. When the coffee arrived he said reluctantly, 'You'd better get Mr Channing on the phone right away.'

Leonard Channing.

Eric had not long since taken his seat on the board of Martin and Channing, merchant bankers in London. The invitation to do so had not been made in the best of spirits.

28

Channing had made it clear that he felt he wanted Eric where he could see him, after they had crossed swords in the matter of the marine insurance claim over the sinking of the *Sea Dawn*. [*Premium on Death*.] Eric had since attended two board meetings and found them deadly boring affairs, with Leonard Channing in the chair acting like a Chinese Tai-Pan. What was even more unsettling, Eric was made patently aware of the fact that the rest of the board regarded him as a complete tyro, taking his seat only by virtue of his wife's investment in the bank. Which was true on both counts, though he had no doubt that they had all bought their way on to the board in some way or another. And knowledge came with experience. He had kept his head down at the meetings, listened and learned.

But he hadn't warmed towards Leonard Channing in any distinct degree. Neither man trusted the other, but distrust didn't necessarily mean dislike: in this case, it did. Eric knew he would be foolish ever to turn his back on Leonard Channing.

The phone rang. Eric waited a moment, then picked it up. 'You're through now, Mr Ward.'

Channing's secretary of course was still on the line. Eric waited patiently while the little power game was played, Eric waiting for Channing to deign to pick up the phone.

'Channing.'

'Leonard, you rang me. I'm returning the call.'

There was a short pause. 'My dear boy, yes, thank you. How are you? A restful sojourn in the Northumberland countryside?'

'Very much so.'

'I didn't ring you at Sedleigh Hall because although it was urgent I hesitated to break in on your peace and relaxation. How is Anne, by the way?'

'Fine.'

'Tell her we're still looking after her investments, we workers down here in the City.' Channing chuckled gratingly, gravel and sandpaper with no hint of sincerity. But the point was made.

'What can I do for you, Leonard?'

There was a short silence, as though Channing was considering. 'Something's come up, Ward, and although you're still a very junior member of the board of Martin and Channing, I think it would be a good idea if you got involved. I mean, it would help you bloody yourself a bit in the bank's affairs, get you a bit of useful experience, and it would in addition make you feel you're keeping an active eye on your wife's investments.'

Eric ignored the dig. 'What's it all about?'

'We'll be holding a meeting in a couple of days' time,' Channing said urbanely, 'and while I realize it's short notice, I gather you

30

don't have too much on at the little office on the Quayside, so do you think you could make it, if my secretary gives you the details?'

'If it's important, I can make time,' Eric replied patiently. 'But what's it about?'

'I'll give you all the details when you arrive: a briefing will be prepared. In a nutshell, Ward, we've been asked to help fight off the attack upon the Salamander Corporation—or at least, its English operations, to be more precise. Should be interesting, and it would be a good opportunity for you to get your teeth into something *really* important.'

The underlying sneer remained with Eric after the phone call was terminated. He sat quietly behind his desk, thinking about the call. He didn't trust Leonard Channing. It was perfectly logical to suggest that Eric might play a part in an important contract in order to learn more about the dealings of Martin and Channing, but that would be the case only if Leonard Channing were really interested in helping Eric or building on his existing skills. He wasn't. Eric was under no illusions about the senior partner in the merchant bank: Channing was out to give Eric no helping hand. He would have a reason of his own for asking Eric to get involved—unless, of course, other members of the board had put pressure on. But that was unlikely: they were creatures of Leonard

Channing's, in the main.

The Salamander Corporation.

Eric had seen something about it in the financial press, but the last week or so at Sedleigh Hall had kept him away from latest developments, and he hadn't really paid much attention to the whole business. But he knew someone who would have.

It had begun to rain, a light pattering against the window. Eric shook his head and turned to the other messages on his desk. He dealt with them, one by one, and by early afternoon had cleared the existing pressing business. The rain had stopped, though the clouds above Newcastle were grey and menacing when he left the office, having instructed his secretary to await a call from Channing's secretary to fix the London meeting.

Eric made his way up Grey Street and turned into the narrow lane that led to the offices of the Newcastle subsidiary of Martin and Channing. The sign on the door had now been picked out in gold lettering—Stanley Investments Ltd—but it was one of the few changes that had occurred. The company was no longer moribund, it was true, no longer a dumping ground for Martin and Channing's embarrassing contracts, and to Reuben Podmore's pleasure it was actively trading again. Nevertheless the office was still a small one, meagrely furnished, barely adequately staffed and making only the slightest concessions to modern technology.

But that was the way Reuben Podmore wanted it. 'If you look too affluent, Mr Ward, northern businessmen won't deal through you. They're canny folk, but they watch their pockets, so it's better to keep a low profile and give a good service.'

He'd been in the business long enough to know, so Eric had bowed to his advice. Since the *Sea Dawn* affair the board of Martin and Channing had left the firm to Eric's guidance—he in turn relied upon Podmore, of course. Strictly speaking, however, Eric was in control: his one really active involvement in Anne's affairs, since it was her investment that had bought the seat on Martin and Channing and control of Stanley Investments.

''Morning, Mr Podmore.'

'A pleasure to see you, Mr Ward.' Though not entirely, Eric thought, smiling to himself. Podmore's face always reflected a mixture of emotions when he greeted Eric: gratitude for the assistance he had given the man in Pink Lane some years ago, pleasure at the liking that had sprung up between them, respect for the way they had together defeated Leonard Channing over the marine insurance claim in the *Sea Dawn* affair, but anxiety that Eric was possibly about to bring more problems of an equally hazardous nature to disturb the equanimity of Podmore's life. He did have his heart to think about, after all.

'You're well, Reuben?'

'As well as a frail old man can expect,' Podmore replied, settling his bulk back behind his desk. He caressed his jowls thoughtfully as he inspected Eric. 'You look rested.'

'A few days off. But now back to business. And guess who calls me as soon as I get back?'

'Guessing is for amateurs, Mr Ward. In the business of finance one takes calculated risks.'

'Leonard Channing.'

'Ah.' It was a pregnant sound, emphasized by the twist of Podmore's mouth. The financial manager of Stanley Investments did not care for Leonard Channing.

'So talk to me about the Salamander Corporation.'

'*Salamander?*' Reuben's little eyes widened and his pendulous lower lip was thrust out in an expression of surprise. 'You are to be involved?'

'It seems so. But involved in what? I know very little about Salamander. I thought you'd be able to fill me in.'

'So, tell you about the Salamander Corporation.' Reuben Podmore wrinkled his nose and shrugged. 'Where to begin?'

'At the best place?'

Podmore smiled. 'For the beginning, one

34

must go back to the takeover cycle that began on Wall Street after the recession in 1980. Raiders captured Getty, Gulf and the other big oil companies. Since then, the raiders have moved on into the industrial heartland of America. And you know what's at stake, Mr Ward?'

'Tell me.'

'The whole industrial landscape of America. And for merchant banks, it's important business. You see, corporate raiders, predatory companies who buy up others to restructure them, they all resort to the same answer when they hit financing problems. They issue bonds.' Podmore half closed his eyes reflectively. 'And you can look back to the 1840s in England to see the dangers. The railway boom then destroyed a lot of fortunes—as well as making some. Many people today consider that the bonds that are now issued could go the same way as the nineteenth-century railway bonds. They'll end up as junk.'

'What's this got to do with Salamander?'

'A little patience, Mr Ward. It is necessary you understand how Salamander came into being. Essentially, it is a child of its time.'

Eric settled back in his chair. 'Go on.'

'I do not wish to suggest that raiders are simply unscrupulous financiers who enjoy profiting from the human misery caused by the redundancies their actions provoke. The

35

world is not so black and white. Takeovers are not simply asset-stripping exercises.'

Eric nodded. He thought back to the acquisition exercise Anne was entering into: in a smaller way, it was carrying out a corporate raid, but the thrust behind it was not merely financial: it would be driven by a sense that operating efficiencies could be achieved.

'But any takeover boom,' Podmore continued, 'will depend upon a bull market. If the cash dries up, the raiders retire. On the other hand, there'll still be investors happy to buy the junk bonds that have been issued, in the hope that better times will return.'

'Do they?'

Podmore smiled. 'Oddly enough, they do. But it *is* a risk.'

Eric considered the matter. 'But how do you recognize a junk bond?'

'It's a bond that's below its investment grade. The first investment bank to spot the potential of such bonds was Drexel Burnham Lambert. They still have more than a hundred billion dollars' worth of the market.'

'Are you saying that *big* investors buy junk?'

'The banks reckon there's about sixty big institutional investors willing to take them. You see, the fact is, in spite of the gloomy predictions, junk bonds have on the whole disproved their below-investment-grade tag.

The risks are certainly higher—more in the nature of a bet upon the company's business than a stake in a corporate bond.'

'But they've still shown a good return?' Eric asked.

'Twelve per cent, against a Treasury rate of just over seven.'

'So let's get down to it, Reuben. How does the Salamander Corporation fit into this picture?'

Reuben Podmore sighed, and spread his hands wide. 'A classical story. I believe the original bank had a much less colourful name—somewhere out in the mid-west USA. They were in the business of corporate finance but not in any large way, until an oil-rich Texan called Paul Everett came on the scene. He bought out the bank, and not a moment too soon. The oil crisis developed, some of his own oil investments crashed, a couple of dry fields turned up—he could have been in trouble. But he got out rapidly and in fact made it into the big time again. But not in oil—in corporate finance.'

'How?'

'Would you like some coffee? So much talking, it makes me dry, like Everett's oil fields. *Margaret!*' He ordered the coffee and sat down again, perspiring slightly. 'I am getting too fat again, so I must take my coffee black, and decaffeinated, of course.'

'I understand. Salamander,' Eric said

firmly.

'But of course. Salamander—so Everett with his new company made it into the big time financially by lending money to finance their clients' takeover bids. They then helped in the issue and placing of junk bonds to finance those bids—many of which were successful in the post 1980's boom. In turn, Salamander wisely invested a considerable part of its own capital in those junk bonds, and also in certain highly leveraged companies where the return on the equity was often astronomical.'

'You're talking of big business.'

'*Big*,' Podmore agreed. 'In 1984 Salamander used a million dollars of its capital to help Morgan's buy a fifty per cent stake in Nicholas Holdings. It serves as a good example of the Salamander technique. Half of the money was up front, from Salamander's own borrowings. The second half was a delayed payment.'

'And?'

Podmore smiled. 'The delayed payment never became necessary. Interest rates and improved company performance pushed up share prices. Salamander got a large slice in fees, of course, but by using its saved profits it also bought into Nicholas Holdings at just the right time. It's the key to the success of Salamander. Everett always showed an uncanny aptitude to buy at the right time.'

Eric nodded. 'But as I understand it, Salamander is now under some pressure.'

Podmore nodded. 'Not for the first time. The fact is, Everett learned the hard truth in the States. There is no company that's too big to be taken over. *Any* company can be taken over, broken up, remoulded. And Everett's success was too quick. He made enemies—not just his wives.'

'*Wives?*'

Podmore looked vaguely unhappy, as though wishing he had not mentioned the matter. It was gossip, not financial management. 'He's been married three times. It has cost him a couple of fortunes in alimony. He has a reputation as a womanizer: a girl in every capital. But the big enemies were those who sought to emulate his financial methods. Namely, corporate raiders saw what he had done and determined to do the same to him. Salamander was the subject of several bids.'

'But if he was so big—'

'Size is irrelevant,' Podmore insisted. 'In this kind of climate a minnow can swallow a whale, by obtaining credit, by issuing junk, by making the shareholders offers they can't refuse. Of course, some of the raiders simply pushed up Salamander share prices by their bids, sold out their own holdings at a profit and disappeared. But it left Salamander in trouble: Everett had been forced to match bids, buy his own shares, and his position in liquid terms was severely weakened. On top of that—'

'There was more?' There was a tap on the door, and Podmore's secretary, a middle-aged lady with hornrimmed spectacles and an ample bosom on which she balanced the tray, entered. 'Ah, the coffee.'

Podmore looked at his own black liquid and sighed, watching Eric add milk to his own. 'I dislike black coffee. Do you know it rots the teeth? However . . . Everett had diversified, of course, but hit anti-trust actions just at a time when another corporate raider made a firm bid for his empire. The dollar was also weakening badly, and the story is Everett decided to call it a day in USA terms. He sold out, to the surprise of all, caught the raiders off balance and moved the whole business to London, where he had already registered Salamander under English company law.'

'He went into the same business?' Eric asked.

'It was a business he now knew intimately. But maybe some of the aggressive edge has been lost in the last five years. He does not hold the confidence in the City that he held on Wall Street. And history is repeating itself.'

'He's been threatened by a raider?'

'The most vulnerable kind of company is

one in which the management has lost credibility. The question is asked: are the shares trading at below true net asset value? If they are, the people who hold those shares will be willing to sell. This is the position with Salamander now. Everett's flight from the States looked like a cut and run. The raiders are now after him in England. Salamander is the subject of an attack from Gower and Rue and they've put together a powerful bid. It's why Paul Everett has brought in Hugh Nelson as a consultant.'

'Hugh Nelson?'

'The arbitrageur.' Podmore smiled. 'Interesting, isn't it? And now Martin and Channing will be putting together the financial package in defence.'

★   ★   ★

'So what's so interesting, bringing in an arbitrageur?' Anne asked. 'I don't understand the point.'

Eric lay on his back on the close-cropped turf above the mass of contorted whinstone below. He watched the hawk, hovering in the blue sky, wings trembling in the light breeze, scanning the stony channels and the scrub of the crags on the height up which Eric and Anne had ridden, down to the sprouting waves of fern on the lower slopes.

'The point is, Salamander have bought in

the kind of talent that normally they'd find a threat. An arbitrageur makes his living by buying a large block of shares in a company that's at the receiving end of a takeover bid. Since it's in his interests to sell those shares to the highest bidder, he'll be deaf to any appeals from the defending company.'

'Does he have any stake in Salamander?'

'Who knows? My guess is, Salamander is afraid he might step in—so they've bought him out of the action. He has quite a reputation on the City scene—no heart, and a fine sense of timing. Also a smooth line in talk: he describes what he does as *providing liquidity in the market*. Defending companies see him differently—as a ravening shark.'

'Would it be worth while this man Nelson giving up the chance to play the market? I mean, would his fee from Salamander compensate?' Anne asked.

'I doubt it. But he's probably been offered some other slice of the action—maybe an equity in the defending company. I don't know. I guess I'll find out more about it when I get to the meeting on Monday.'

Seated beside him, chewing on a piece of grass, Anne was silent for a few minutes. Some thirty yards away their two mounts grazed, tethered to the scrub. Beyond them the hog's back of Cheviot rose, heather-strewn, patched with silky tufts of cotton grass. 'Did I tell you Jim Edmonds has been on the phone again?'

Eric made no reply, and after a short silence Anne went on. 'He's made the initial contact with Roger Graham. They've agreed to meet us to open discussions, with no commitment either side, of course. Will you be able to come to the meeting?'

'Depends when it is.'

'You'll probably get to meet the fabulous Karen O'Neill.'

'It's to be a social gathering?' Eric asked, shading his eyes to look at Anne.

'Social-business, I guess, to pretend none of us are really seriously bothered about the outcome. You know how it works.'

'If I come . . .'

'I know,' Anne said, a trifle testily. 'It's without commitment that you'll get involved.'

'Martin and Channing is *your* involvement,' Eric pointed out. 'If I get tied in with this Graham affair as well, I'll have no time for my own practice in Newcastle.'

For a moment he thought Anne was about to respond, but she clearly thought better of it. He was aware of her feelings about the practice: a bit of commercial law, a reputation on the criminal practice side, it was never going to be a gold-lined business, but it was what he enjoyed doing, it retained his independence, and somehow it kept him in touch with the side of life he had grown up with—Tyneside, the police force, law. And it was law that had kept him sane at the roughest time in his life, when he had been alone, facing blindness.

Relenting, he said, 'I'll help in any way I can, love. Much depends upon what this Salamander thing demands of me. We'll see how it goes, okay?'

The hawk had gone. A swallow-glide away, black grouse began to cackle again in the heather.

*   *   *

The offices of the Salamander Corporation occupied four floors of a glass tower in west London. Its brochures mentioned that it owned all thirty floors of the building with its views of the glistening snake of the Thames. Fronting the offices was a piazza, Italianate in style: the theme continued inside the building itself, the entrance hall being an extention of the piazza, air-conditioned, with water flowing down one wall over a sheet of glittering mineral that transformed the flow into a million points of variegated light.

Dark-suited men, security officers, wandered with a studied sharp-eyed nonchalance at the fringes of the entrance hall. The reception desk was staffed by two girls chosen for beauty and presence as well as ability. Eric ignored them. He knew which

44

floor to head for. He walked towards the escalator, which took him to the mezzanine level and the lifts. No security man intercepted him: he had no doubt they had been briefed and would already have recognized him.

The bare floors echoed to his footsteps: the marble was smooth, hard and cold, not unlike Paul Everett, he understood. He reached the lift: a sign warned that it was under electronic surveillance. Eric reminded himself not to pick his nose in its privacy.

Inside the lift he noted the video lens in the roof: someone would be watching the top of his head as he was whisked rapidly to the twentieth floor of the Salamander building.

The brisk secretary who greeted him as he left the lift was no surprise: security would have warned her that Eric Ward was on the way. She smiled brightly. 'The others have already arrived, sir. Would you come this way?' Eric checked his watch. It was just on two-fifteen. He wouldn't have put it past Leonard Channing to set him up as fifteen minutes late.

In the event, he decided the thought was an unworthy one. When he was ushered into the palatial office of Paul Everett it was clear that the meeting had not yet started.

The room was dominated by a massive desk placed near the curving windows, offering a view of the river and the skyline of

London. The drapes were heavy silk, cream in colour, subtly patterned; the boardroom table glistened, the carpet was thick, the paintings on the walls were originals—a Matisse, two Cézannes. The girl who sat quietly to the left of the door would be recording the meeting, Eric had no doubt: she was also most decorative, with a lissom figure and a welcoming smile.

Leonard Channing was moving casually towards him, waving a languid hand, elegant, dark-suited. 'Ah, Eric, although this isn't my meeting, so to speak, perhaps I should undertake the introductions, in the circumstances.' He inclined his head towards the big man who stood with his back to the window. 'This is Paul Everett, managing director of Salamander.'

And its major shareholder. Eric shook his hand. The man was over six feet in height, broad-shouldered and in his early fifties. He carried little excess weight: Eric had heard he showed a commitment to exercise in his private gym that was matched only by his approach to business. His hair was still dark, with wings of grey at the sides and his eyebrows were shaggy, forming a black ridge above a dominant nose. He held his head to one side as he was introduced to Eric, like a wise old blackbird sizing up a worm. His mouth was sensuous, but held a hint of cruelty, and Eric was not drawn to the man:

46

his handshake was non-committal, as though he feared giving something away, and his eyes were flat and grey, cold in their appraisal, hard in their assessment.

'And may I introduce you to Hugh Nelson?'

A spare man, of middle height, carefully dressed, his bright tie being the only hint of the flamboyance he was credited with in the City, Nelson was in his late thirties and was waiting for no man. His manner was crisp, his warm brown eyes alight with a nervous tension that would merely reflect the fires that burned inside him. He had made a considerable reputation for himself in the City and elsewhere; a bachelor, he was rumoured to like fast women and faster cars, but allowed neither to interfere with his business. He would never stand out in a crowd in physical terms, but in a small gathering like this, Eric guessed, he could soon become dominant by his sheer intellect and force of argument.

'It's the first time I've met an arbitrageur,' Eric said, smiling.

Nelson returned the smile; it was warm, and friendly. 'It derives from the French *arbitrer*: to judge, estimate, arbitrate. It just means we're accommodating guys, always willing to settle the differences between warring parties.'

'Not quite how many in the city would

describe you,' Everett commented, with an edge to his voice. Nelson looked at him, retaining the smile but dropping its warmth. 'I don't listen to City gossip,' he replied. 'I *make* it.'

Curious bedfellows, Eric thought: the arbitrageur and the financier. Everett would hardly welcome Nelson to his boardroom when he would inevitably see him as the opportunist who profited from imperfections in the money system, so there must be strong reasons for his presence.

Everett grunted and turned away, walked to the table and sat down. The girl near the door pressed a bell on the wall: seconds later the door opened and a tray of coffee was brought in as the others sat down at the table. Everett was silent for several long minutes; no one else attempted to speak. At last he placed the tips of his fingers together, and a little sourly announced, 'This is your party, Channing. You'd better get it started.'

Leonard Channing was unmoved by Everett's characteristic sharpness. He nodded, drew a cup of coffee towards him and said, 'Thank you, Paul. I'm grateful for this opportunity to meet you and Nelson. I've already explained to you the reason for Ward's presence.'

It was more than he had done for Eric.

'The concept of a war cabinet,' he continued, 'now seems to me to be necessary.

You have received the details of the financial package we have put together for you as a defensive measure against the bid of Gower and Rue. It takes full account of the share price offer they made and the package they tied in with it. You'll recall that the Gower-Rue bid was cleared as acceptable by the Department of Trade and Industry; the counter-bid we prepared for you offered your shareholders a better deal to persuade them to hold tight and support the present board under your chairmanship.'

'That's all old hat,' Everett interrupted, shaking his head, 'ever since Gower-Rue put in their new bid on Monday.'

'Which is why I suggested the war cabinet meeting, and the involvement of Mr Nelson,' Channing said urbanely, raising his chin slightly and meeting Everett's surly gaze. 'I'm here in an advisory capacity from Martin and Channing, Paul, and if you don't like what I'm telling you that's your privilege as a client, but I would be forsaking my duty if I did not tell you what you need to be told. Eric is here as a member of my board to keep me straight on the legalities; but Nelson brings to this war cabinet a new element—of surprise and entrepreneurship, and of imaginative counter-attack.'

'At a price,' Everett grunted.

'It's opportunity cost, not marginal cost we're talking about here,' Nelson remarked, leaning back confidently in his chair. 'If you think I come cheap, you're wrong.'

'I'll want results for the money.'

'I always bring in results.'

'To your own advantage.'

'This time, to yours, since you're paying.'

'Gentlemen, please,' Channing intervened. 'I think this is a discussion we've already had, separately and together, behind closed doors. We've no need to go over it again now. Agreement has been reached; we're together as a war cabinet to fight off the Gower-Rue "final" bid—a bid of some consequence. We now know the kind of fight we have to put up. The question is, what form does it take? Nelson is here to advise, you to approve, Paul, since it's your company. Me, I merely act as honest broker who will then put together the defensive financial package you want.'

There was a short silence. They all waited for Everett to speak. He didn't; finally, he merely nodded, with a studied and deliberate reluctance. He didn't like Hugh Nelson or what the man stood for, and he didn't like him in his boardroom. Channing sighed.

'So, Nelson, what kind of counter-bid do we now put together to fight off Gower-Rue?'

Hugh Nelson had quite small hands: he studied them now with care, as though seeing their structure and texture for the first time. 'I think the time is already past for a defence

50

of Salamander.'

'What the hell is that supposed to mean?' Everett almost snarled. 'Is that the kind of advice I'm paying for?'

Nelson ignored him. He looked at Eric, the uncommitted lawyer in a highly charged atmosphere. 'Risk arbitrage, which is what I'm good at, exploits the differences which exist between securities with a fixed relationship—such as the terms upon which they can be switched from convertible to ordinary shares; that relationship becomes heightened in a takeover bid. In making my decision to dive in, I look at certain key factors.'

Eric glanced towards Everett; the managing director of Salamander had cooled since his brief outburst of temper. But his calm was the more dangerous: his glance was locked on Nelson, like a serpent ready to strike.

'I ask myself,' Nelson continued, 'whether the merger would make sense, how valuable the acquired company would be, how badly the managements want the fight, how well is the merger being handled, and how compatible the business is with general merger activity at that time. I've listed the factors; I've applied them to this game we have on hand. I've reached my conclusions. *I* would dive into this takeover, assuredly—if *Mr* Everett hadn't made it worth my while with his fee and share package offer. And if I *had* dived in, I'd have backed Gower-Rue right down the line.'

'*Why?*' Everett hadn't moved but the question came like a whipcrack.

Hugh Nelson remained unimpressed. 'This company is over the hill in progressive terms. It needs a change of management. You're getting out of touch, Everett; you ran from trouble in the States, but the hounds are gathering over here now. They want to do some asset-stripping, of course, but they'll also reconstruct this company and make it a leaner, fitter business, with a higher profitability level within three years.'

'I can whip Salamander into shape.'

'Sure you can, but *will* you? Do you have the clear incentive? Women and wine and the soft life don't match up to the modern—'

'Gentlemen—' Channing tried to interrupt.

'It surprises me you agreed to come in, and take shares in Salamander,' Everett said viciously, ignoring Channing, 'if you see the company as underachieving.'

'Oh, don't get me wrong,' Nelson said cheerfully. 'Once we've beaten off Gower and Rue and settled the market place I'm certain Salamander shares will rise. I'll be holding my package: I'll not stay with you, but sell at the best price. Who knows, I might even start a new attack upon you—'

'You bastard—'

'*But the first job is to beat off Gower and Rue!*'

'And you've already said you'd have swung in with them! Defeatist!'

The two men glared at each other. Eric was fascinated. Neither man had raised his voice in the interchange. They had delivered their statements, explained their positions quietly, coldly and without open rancour in their tones. Behind the words lay bitter enmity, but Eric was beginning to realize what a masterstroke Channing had produced, throwing the two men together.

He guessed both Nelson and Everett knew it, too, and were merely fencing, searching out weakness for future reference.

'So where do we go from here?' Channing asked.

Nelson shrugged. 'Salamander is in a classical position. I believe its shares are—or were—trading below net asset value. Salamander has had two options open to it—cut operating costs and boost the share price higher by selling assets to buy in their shares—what we call restructuring. Or there's the alternative: do nothing. That's what Salamander has done: nothing. It's OK as a strategy, but it's high risk, and it's now too late to restructure. Too expensive, with the share price already boosted by the Gower-Rue bid.'

'So we just lie on our backs?' Everett

asked.

'I've already spoken to Channing. He's put together a counter-bid—a mix of shares and cash incentive. It might pull in the investors to support you. I don't think it will.'

'It's an offer which improves upon Gower-Rue,' Channing objected.

'But not significantly enough. You'll get some early selling—entrepreneurs taking their profits and running, small investors short of a bit of cash. But you won't have cracked the problem.'

'So what do *you* propose!' Everett demanded. 'Let's see some action for the fee.'

Nelson gazed blandly at the head of the Salamander Corporation. 'No. I've no advice at this stage. I want to see the reaction to Channing's package in the market. And I want immediate access to all relevant information behind the accounts.'

'To hell with you,' Everett stated evenly, but with a determined malice in his voice. 'You must think I'm crazy.'

'You ought to be *desperate*,' Nelson rejoined. 'And sensible enough to realize I'm on your side—'

'For now!'

'—and that the kind of information I'll dig out wouldn't be much use to me later when it's all over.'

'Except in a law court!' Everett snapped.

Nelson smiled. 'A chance you have to take.

Except maybe what I recommend as a result of that information being supplied to me would be a sufficient gun for you to hold against my head.'

Something tingled against Eric's spine as he watched Everett take the remark, let it sink in, and then gradually relax. A touch of vulpine amusement became visible on his mouth, slowly, as he stared at Nelson and the arbitrageur held his gaze. Something was going on that Eric only dimly understood: the two financiers were of a mind, they knew the implications of Nelson's stand. Eric did not. He looked at Channing. The urbane, patrician profile of the senior partner in Martin and Channing was unreadable.

Channing raised his head. 'I have here the financial package we've been talking about—the shares and cash deal. I've also prepared a statement of the bond issues you might have to make in due course to finance the purchase of our shareholders' loyalty. Perhaps if we could now look at these in a little more detail and I'll explain the structure and timing of the issues . . .'

Later, as he stepped into the taxi with Leonard Channing, Eric considered that the last hour spent in going over those details with Channing had not been the most important period in the meeting. There was a strange air of going through the motions: they were considering the information against a darker background. It was as though both Everett and Nelson had come to some private agreement on strategy in which Channing's package would be seen only as a feint, a skirmish to draw the fangs of the enemy. The package was *important*, that was clear; on the other hand, he was left with the impression that both financiers knew that bloodier action lay ahead.

Eric settled in the taxi beside Channing. After Channing gave directions to the driver, he said, 'No company car today?'

'Gives the wrong impression to the client,' Channing said with a wintry smile.

'And what impression did *my* introduction make to the client?'

'I don't know what you mean, Ward.'

'And I don't know what the hell I was doing there.'

'As a member of the board of Martin and Channing you—'

Eric cut him short. 'That's rubbish, and you know it.'

There was a short silence. At last, Channing inclined his head gracefully. 'All right. You're entitled to know.' He paused. 'Your presence on the board has been noted, as has your inclination to . . . listen and learn. Certain senior members of the board now believe it is time you took more responsibility for board action than hitherto. You are legally qualified—the only board

member so qualified. It's time you used your
. . . skills, to the benefit of Martin and
Channing.'

The tone was sincere, but still something
rang not quite true. 'I'm not a company
lawyer, Channing.'

'There is another matter. Members of the
board know of your background . . . the
police, not least of all. They feel you might
possess, from that background, a certain
ability to . . . recognize suspicious
circumstances, the possibility of defalcation.
It's not a view I support, though I do grant
you a certain low cunning . . .'

This was more like the real Channing, Eric
thought grimly. 'It still doesn't quite explain
my involvement with the Salamander affair.'

'You'll be there to listen, learn, and protect
the back of Martin and Channing. You'll be
the legal officer—the compliance officer if you
like—who'll make sure we don't offend the
Department of Trade and Industry. You'll be
aware they're like hunting wolves at the
moment, slavering at the doors of most City
institutions.'

Protecting the public interest, was the way
Eric would have put it.

'However, I'll be drawing up a
memorandum of our discussion today. It will
be of restricted circulation, of course, and will
not be available to members of the board at
this time. Later, naturally, it will become

common property. I'll draw it up as a record of the discussion and if you would be kind enough to sign it as an accurate account . . . I get out here. You'll be returning to Newcastle, Ward?'

And be glad to, Eric thought, still uneasy about his position in the Salamander affair.

3

'Darling, can you do me up?'

Eric wandered into the bedroom. Anne had decided to wear a simple white sheath dress this evening and it showed off her figure to perfection. He zipped up the dress for her and she turned and kissed him lightly. 'You're not ready yet?'

'Won't take me long. I'll just finish reading the newspaper—'

'Well, don't leave it till the last minute. The car is calling for us at eight, and we're picking up Edmonds at eight-fifteen. Do you think she'll turn up this time?'

'Who?'

'Karen O'Neill!'

'The woman of mystery. I guess so. If she doesn't your acquisitions expert will throw a fit.'

Eric walked back into the sitting-room and picked up the newspaper. He turned to the financial section. He had started to read a brief report when Anne had called.

DTI START DEALING PROBE

The City was wriggling with embarrassment today at the suggestion that recent clean-ups have still left some dirty laundry to be washed. Last month's swoop on financier Reeves Grenham and the disclosure that two million in shares had been wiped off the account as a result of company peccadilloes seems not to be the end of the story.

DTI sources revealed today that further investigations are not ruled out. In particular, the movement of certain shares immediately prior to the Reeves Grenham wipeout, and selling that went on through a series of off-shore transactions are raising the question yet again: has the City Code really got any teeth? The rules against insider dealing are clear enough. In the old days the City followed its own code of practice because it *was* the City. Now, things have changed: there's a new breed of pike in the millpond. The gentlemanly days are long since gone, and the new entrepreneurs stick at nothing.

The DTI seem determined to keep probing—but who will be found to have sticky fingers next?

Eric folded up the paper thoughtfully. He walked across to the window and looked out over the darkening Newcastle skyline. A golden glow hung above the distant coast, the last fading of the dying sun. Up at Sedleigh Hall the swifts would be whirling and darting . . .

He shook his head. He had been softened by those last few days of early summer up at their home in Northumberland. Tonight it was business again, if in the guise of a social get-together at Perastino's Restaurant.

It had been the suggestion of Roger Graham himself that they should meet at Perastino's. They would be in a relatively quiet part of the city, would have a private room to themselves, and would be able both to get to know each other better and open up the conversations Edmonds had already initiated. Wives would be present—though neither Nick nor Chris Graham were married—and the occasion would have at least the façade of relaxation. The tensions below might run sharply, nevertheless.

As for Anne, she seemed more interested in whether the fabulous Karen O'Neill would turn up than in her first encounter with the supposedly redoubtable Roger Graham.

The car arrived promptly and whisked them off to the flat Edmonds kept on the outskirts of the city. He was ready and waiting. When he joined them in the car he made a perfunctory attempt at conversation but it was clear that he was edgy again: Eric could guess it would be his fiancée rather than

60

the projected business that would be bothering him. Edmonds had control of his professional life, it seemed, but his social situation gnawed at his self-confidence.

They arrived at Perastino's some fifteen minutes later. A taxi was already drawing up at the restaurant in front of them. Edmonds craned his neck and then, almost before the car had stopped he was opening the door and jumping out. He almost ran towards the woman standing beside the taxi and she turned to look at him, startled, then smiling.

'It would seem the myth has turned to reality,' Anne murmured.

When they got inside the restaurant Eric was able to appreciate the reason for Edmonds's obsession. Karen O'Neill was tall, with green eyes and light auburn hair. She moved lithely, and her tanned skin seemed to glow. There was something provocative about her features, a challenging lift to her chin as she spoke to a man, a natural coquettishness, but her handshake was firm and positive. Eric guessed that beautiful as she was, her beauty was matched by her intelligence . . . or perhaps something else. When he was introduced a shadow moved subtly deep in her green eyes and she held his hand just a fraction too long.

'My God,' Anne said in a stricken voice to Eric, as they moved in ahead of Edmonds and his fiancée, 'she's *gorgeous*!'

'It's the make-up,' Eric assured her, and received a dig in the ribs for his pains.

There were perhaps fifteen people in the private room that had been booked for them. Several of them were senior employees of Roger Graham, Ltd, members of the management team. They would be there to add to the social emphasis, with their wives in tow: the group to the left were the ones who really mattered. Edmonds introduced them.

'Roger Graham and Mrs Graham; Nick Graham and Miss Frain; Chris Graham.'

Miss Frain was decoration, a well-developed young lady who probably served Nick Graham's needs from time to time without impinging upon his life too seriously. Roger Graham's wife was a Byker girl, now in her sixties, and clearly still uncertain how she and her husband had got where they were. Eric considered maybe she wished they never had got there: she seemed uneasy, particularly when she stood beside the glittering Miss Frain.

Roger Graham was short, stocky and pugnacious. He was completely bald and the recent sunshine had reddened his scalp, causing the skin to peel. He was powerful in his upper arms and shoulders, but the years had redistributed his weight somewhat, and he had become corpulent. His recent heart attack had jolted some of the weight from him, Eric guessed, but it had cost him none of his natural belligerence. His lips were half hidden by a grey moustache and he wore his sideburns unfashionably long. 'So you're Ward,' he grunted. 'Heard of you. Quayside, isn't it? Not many lawyers down there.'

'Maybe that's why I like it,' Eric said, smiling.

'This is Nick Graham,' Jim Edmonds said. 'Mr and Mrs Ward.'

Nick Graham was taller than his father. He was perhaps fifty years of age, maybe slightly younger, and he had inherited his father's pugnacity of feature while managing to control the belligerence more effectively. He had snapping dark eyes, ever shifting: on being introduced to Eric he glanced at him, summed him up, then flickered towards Anne as though recognizing that it was she who was important to him, rather than Eric. It was an impression Eric was happy to support. This was Anne's business.

'I've been looking forward to meeting you,' Nick Graham said to Anne, and sounded as though he meant it. He was clearly at ease with women, and prepared to make use of charm even in business situations. Anne liked him, Eric thought as he watched her: a good enough start to what might be difficult negotiations.

Eric had stepped back slightly to take a soft drink from the tray offered him. Edmonds was turning towards Chris Graham, to introduce him in his turn, and as he did so Eric caught a glimpse of Karen O'Neill. She was frowning. It was gone in a moment but it had been there, and she had been looking at Chris Graham. Eric stepped forward to be introduced and the youngest member of the Graham entourage shook his hand. The man's glance slipped past Eric, nevertheless, almost involuntarily, to Karen O'Neill.

Eric observed them as they were introduced. Once again he received the impression that the girl held Graham's hand just a second too long, though this time there was reluctance on Graham's part to release the handshake. They were much of a height, Chris Graham's eyes on a level with Karen O'Neill's, but there seemed to be a certain tension between them. As she turned away with Edmonds, to speak to Roger Graham and his wife, Chris Graham took a whisky and then watched them. He had fair hair, long-lashed, almost feminine eyes, completely unlike his brother or father. He was slim, but well-muscled and he moved lightly, with an athletic grace.

'Beach boy type,' Anne whispered in Eric's ear.

'They don't have beach boys on the Northumberland coast. Too cold.'

'They do too. They just don't stay in the water too long, that's all. But what I meant is he's the *type*—you know, golden-boy muscles

64

and all that. Likes himself.'

With no time for his father's business. Eric was inclined to agree: there was the hint of the butterfly about Chris Graham. He would see his father's business as a key to enjoying life, where Nick Graham was different: for him the business would *be* life. Nick would not have married because of the business; Chris . . . maybe thirty-five, thirty-eight years old . . . would not have married because life was too good to marry. It was a thought.

They wandered, groups changed in composition, the buffet was served, wine began to flow freely, the noise levels began to rise. Music intervened, softly at first, then more loudly and laughter became more frequent, and noticeable.

'Roger Graham wants to talk,' Anne said in a low voice as she glided past Eric. 'You'll join us?'

'Will Edmonds?'

Eric nodded towards the financial adviser, trapped for the moment with Mrs Graham, but making no secret of his anxiety as he watched his fiancée, standing in one corner of the room, her back to the wall. Leaning close to her, talking urgently, was Chris Graham, glass in one hand, supporting himself with his left hand against the wall beside her head. He seemed flushed, and excited about something.

As Eric watched, Nick Graham joined his

brother and Karen O'Neill. He spoke briefly to him and Chris turned his head, glared defiantly at his brother and pointedly turned his back. He took up his conversation with Edmonds's fiancée, and after a moment, shoulders set angrily, Nick Graham turned away, stumped back towards where his father sat at a table near the door. 'Let's join the club,' Anne suggested, humming discordantly. 'It's not going to be a happy night.'

Jim Edmonds's face said the same when he joined them at the table. He sat down, half-turned, so he could keep half an eye on the still urgently talking Chris Graham.

Roger Graham lit a cigar his doctor had probably advised him against, drew on it, and said to Nick, 'He not joining us?'

'In his own time, I expect.'

His father grunted. 'No matter. Well then, Mrs Ward, I was always noted for my bluntness. Should have been a Yorkshireman, not a Geordie, I'm told. You're interested in my company.'

'As you're interested in talking about it.'

Roger Graham grinned sourly. 'Talking about it, but not giving it away.'

'Who's talking money?'

'You're talking takeover!'

'A merger of interest, I would have said.' She was cool, Eric thought admiringly, and she was not going to be browbeaten by the old

66

man.

He glanced back across the room towards Chris Graham. Karen O'Neill had straightened, placed a hand on Graham's arm, as though she were trying to step away from him. Chris Graham was still talking rapidly, gesticulating, and Jim Edmonds's hands were tense on the table. He was paying little attention to the conversation between Roger Graham and Anne.

'One of the key things we'd need to know, of course,' Anne was saying, 'is to what extent you would wish the existing management to play a part in the company in future.'

'We'd be very positive about that,' Roger Graham insisted. 'There's no way I'd want to see my company carved up. I've confidence in Nick—'

'But just hold your horses,' Nick Graham intervened. 'We've not even said we're interested in talking merger yet.'

'Acquisition,' Anne corrected quietly. 'I think we should speak plainly from the beginning and not blur issues with soft words.'

'Mrs Ward,' Nick Graham replied, his voice tightening, 'I don't care what you call it. There are no strings attached to this meeting. It's merely an exploration, to determine whether the two companies concerned wish to pursue . . . possibilities.

But let's clear the air about certain things right now. We're not really interested in sale at this time: I reckon we could be in the market for finance in two years' time, but we have anticipated success to realize right now and there's no reason why we should give that away to an outsider—'

'That's rubbish, and you know it,' Anne said coolly. 'We've got your figures. Mr Edmonds?'

'Er, oh, yes . . .' Edmonds dragged himself away from other considerations at the far end of the room, and glanced awkwardly around the table. 'The . . . the published figures, the profitability levels, your investment needs if you are to retain a sustained level of development in the micro field, all suggest you are under-financed.'

'And you can't realize your *anticipated success* without that financial injection.'

There was a short silence. Nick Graham wanted to speak, but his father's hand was on his arm. The old man needled a glance at Anne, then looked at Eric. He seemed vaguely disturbed, probably by the lead Anne was taking and the positive way she argued. 'You've done your homework, hinny, I'll say that,' he said grudgingly. 'But I like plain talk. So let's put some cards on the table and waste no time. *If*—and it's still a big *if*, whatever your figures might say—we'd be prepared to talk . . . *acquisition*, there are

68

certain things we'd always insist on. A broad price expectation needs to be looked at, of course; existing management would have to be protected—'

'We'd need to know the intentions of your key directors,' Anne interrupted, 'the ones with a significant share-holding.'

Roger Graham nodded, his bald head shining redly in the light. 'There's the type of deal to be decided, the kind of purchase consideration—'

'Performance-related purchase?'

'We wouldn't like that,' Nick Graham intervened sharply. Inadvertently, he too glanced across the room towards Chris Graham. Eric followed his glance. Karen O'Neill had managed to break free of the younger Graham brother; she had attached herself to a small group of company employees, and Graham looked about ready to join his father and brother once he had replenished his whisky.

'We'll need to talk about it,' Anne insisted.

'What else would you want as for now?' Roger Graham asked, his old eyes squeezing almost shut in thought.

'Two things, basically,' Anne replied in an even tone. 'We need to get to know each other better, and learn to trust each other. That means we'll need access to company information. I'd want to put a small investigative team into the company for a short period—'

'Have outsiders snooping around with access to confidential information?' Nick Graham expostulated. A red flush began to stain his face. 'There's no way I can accept that.'

'Without it we can't proceed. I spoke of trust—'

'That would be rip-off!'

'Who's talking of a rip-off?' Chris Graham queried, as he joined them, standing beside his brother's chair.

'An investigative team in the company,' his father said grimly.

'Sounds reasonable to me,' Chris Graham suggested.

'Keep out of this, for God's sake,' Nick Graham snapped. 'You know damn-all about this.'

'I know Morcomb Estates wouldn't want to buy a pig in a poke,' the younger man insisted, waving his whisky glass. 'If you're going to be damn well serious about these . . . *discussions*, at least have the sense to agree what's necessary, without pussyfooting around.'

There was a short silence. The old man glared at his younger son and then shook his head. 'Why I ever . . . ah, to hell with it.' He turned to Anne. 'All right, Mrs Ward, I don't like it but Chris is right. You've got your investigative team.' He ignored the snort of disapproval from Nick Graham. 'What else do you want?'

'Just one more thing. We'd want an assurance that you'll not get involved with other potential purchasers until our own detailed negotiations have been completed.'

'Ah, now that's a different matter,' Chris Graham said loudly. He waved his glass, spilling some of the whisky on the table. He was heading towards inebriation, fuelled by excitement. 'Why the hell should Graham's give you that sort of assurance? Damn it, we want to get the best price we can for the business, and if we can find a higher bidder, then of course we'd want to go for them. Makes sense, doesn't it? And it'll keep you on your toes. Always believe in keeping—'

'Chris doesn't speak for this company,' Roger Graham growled.

'Yes, but hold on, Dad, I still think—'

'*Shut up, Chris!*' Nick Graham put out a hand and gripped his brother's arm. He squeezed, and Eric noted the viciousness in the grip. Chris Graham opened his mouth, staring at his brother, but then gritted his teeth, making no noise, denying the existence of the pain. The malevolence of his gaze was not lost on Eric, however: there was little love lost between the brothers, and Chris Graham would make Nick pay for this petty violence in other ways, when his turn came.

'We did speak of trust,' Anne said quietly.

71

Roger Graham nodded his bald pate. 'All right. No other deals for the moment. Now let's have a drink, for God's sake!'

*   *   *

The old man had been rattled. Whatever he had expected of his negotiations, he had not considered the direct approach that Anne had employed. The smoke from cigars and cigarettes was beginning to affect Eric's eyes; he had taken a couple of glasses of wine and it would be unwise to take more. Anne seemed to be enjoying herself, somewhat lit up by the way she had handled herself at the meeting, and Eric could easily slip away to get some night air. Perastino's boasted a small patio and garden at the back, a stone figurine of Venus and a small fountain and covered walk. Eric strolled out to the patio and stood there, breathing in the soft, early summer air. The sky was a deep blue, the way northern skies were after darkness. From the city there came the distant rumble of traffic.

He heard a step behind him and turned. A cigar glowed; the paunchy form of Roger Graham stood there, inspecting the sky as though he owned it. He seemed to ignore Eric, but when he spoke, it was of Eric's wife.

'She knows what it's about, that woman.'

'I think so.'

'I hadn't expected . . . I thought you'd be

doing the talking. I don't like dealing with women. But with a woman like that . . . a man could have . . .' The old man fell silent, maybe contemplating a past that could have been different, more exciting, with wider horizons. 'Hang on to her.'

Eric smiled. 'I intend to.'

'That other one, now.'

Eric turned. He glanced at Roger Graham. The man was looking back into the room he had just left. Framed in the oblong light was Karen O'Neill, her back to the watchers outside. Her head was back; she was laughing. Eric could not see who she was with.

'She came with you,' Roger Graham announced, almost accusatorily.

'She's engaged to our financial adviser.'

'Edmonds? Yes, of course. You know her well?'

'Met her for the first time this evening. Heard about her modelling career in London, of course.'

'Model?' Roger Graham humphed, stroked his hand over his bald pate and took a stiff pull at the gin and tonic he held. He waved his cigar generally, in vague emphasis. 'Your wife now, she's one thing. That other girl . . . she's another.'

'How do you mean?'

'Trouble. Mrs Ward . . . she's tough. That O'Neill woman, she's hard as nails. Believe it.' He puffed vigorously on his cigar. 'But that's this guy Edmonds's business, right? Our business is different. How much are you involved, Ward?'

'Morcomb Estates is Anne.'

'Yes, but—'

'You'll deal with her.'

Roger Graham was inspecting him carefully in the dim light. He grunted. 'I heard about you, Ward. You're different. Ex-copper, solicitor, not one of the fly boys in the city centre squeezing their clients dry. But then you don't have to, do you? Got a rich wife.'

'That's one explanation,' Eric said evenly.

Graham chuckled wickedly. 'And don't rile easily, either, do you? Cool bastard. But straight, I hear. And your wife isn't just a pretty face, eh?'

'That's for you to decide.'

Roger Graham chuckled again. 'Quite a combination. Work together.' He was silent for a few moments, his mood changing. 'Other families . . . different situations.' His tone was grudging, underlaid with resentment. 'I won't have my company go to the wall, Ward, but I won't have it screwed either. You understand?'

He expected no reply, and received none. The old man humphed again and dragged on his cigar, then turned abruptly, marched back inside.

Eric stayed in the cool of the evening and

74

wondered. Leonard Channing strayed into his thoughts, and the Salamander affair; he mused over Anne's performance; his mind dwelled on Karen O'Neill, and the summation Roger Graham had made of her. Idly, he wondered whether it had been a snap judgement, or something more securely based. In any event it was Edmonds's problem, not his.

The point was well emphasized when they drove back to their respective flats. Eric sat in front with the driver: the two women and Edmonds sat in the back. There was little conversation; the atmosphere almost crackled with tension.

When they got back to the flat, Anne went straight to the bedroom. When he joined her, she was already naked, waiting for him. They made love with an eager passion and afterwards, thinking of her excitement, Eric smiled in the darkness. 'You should go in for acquisitions more often,' he said.

Anne turned, twining her left leg against his, locking her body close to him. 'Huh! So what was turning *you* on, then? Karen O'Neill?'

Oddly, the thought sobered him. He was silent for a while. 'She's bad news, Anne.'

'For Jim Edmonds?' Anne considered the matter. 'I don't know. Maybe he's bad news for her. He's so . . . possessive.'

'They're engaged to be married.'

'Even so. I mean *obsession* . . . did you watch her? She can't take it. I had the feeling in the car, she's going to blow . . .'

And if she did, Eric thought, how would Jim Edmonds take it? A woman and a financial investment, they were both risky adventures; both could ruin your life, but one was more likely to do so than the other.

CHAPTER TWO

1

Anne returned to Sedleigh Hall the following morning prior to taking a trip to Edinburgh for consultations regarding Morcomb Estates and some holdings to be developed north of the border. Eric remained in Newcastle at the flat, and caught up with some of the backlog of work that had arisen during the last few days.

He spent two days in court, largely unproductively, on a civil matter involving the libelling of a local councillor, and a couple of days interviewing and advising clients. It was all pretty run of the mill stuff, although he did manage one afternoon with Ted Grainger offshore, aboard one of Dawson's fleet. There were occasional advantages to having a marine and commercial practice:

certain perquisites did arise from time to time.

There was no point in returning to Sedleigh Hall at the weekend with Anne still in Edinburgh so he relaxed at the flat, sleeping late on the Sunday. He had only just woken up when the phone rang. It was Ted Grainger.

'You seen the papers this morning?'

'I've only just got up.'

'Leading article in *The Times*. You better read it.'

'What's it about?' Eric asked. 'We don't get a newspaper delivery here weekends.'

'It's Salamander,' Grainger replied. 'Gower and Rue have made a new bid, and it's splashed all over the Sunday quality press.'

'Hell's flames,' Eric said. 'I'd better get out. Thanks for calling, Ted.'

Eric dressed quickly after a brief shower and, still unshaven, he left the flat and walked to the nearest newspaper shop at the corner of the next block. Back in the flat he quickly found the article Grainger had mentioned. The headline was thick and black: NEW ATTACK ON SALAMANDER.

Eric sat down and read the article quickly. It began by summarizing the timetable of events that had led up to the present situation. It described how the Salamander Corporation had been built in the States and had then moved its centre of operations to

77

London; filled in with some background on the smaller financial house of Gower and Rue and the sources of the backing for their takeover bid for Salamander, and then highlighted the steps in the chain of events. It began with the launch of the bid, and the rumours that emerged concerning the Salamander defence. The reference of the Gower and Rue bid to the Department of Trade and Industry and its subsequent clearance was dealt with and then comment was made about the Salamander response.

There are elements of uncertainty [Eric read], about just what the Salamander board is doing to fight off its importunate rival. As Gower and Rue snap at the Salamander flanks, the board seems to view the proceedings with a certain disdain, doing very little to persuade shareholders that confidence in the company remains unshaken. True, last week they engaged the services of Martin and Channing, not exactly one of the *leading* merchant bankers in the City, though a respectable and experienced one, to put together a financial package. Rumour has it too that they've engaged a certain arbitrageur—a surprising choice—as adviser. It might be regarded as hooking the sharks before they sink their teeth in. But the defence, when it came, was a low key one. Salamander made a counter-offer to shareholders—a shares plus cash deal. Attractive in itself, nevertheless it was almost bound to draw from Gower and Rue a further attack—and this weekend it was launched. In an open letter to shareholders Gower and Rue have launched a new, improved and 'final' bid.

The question's obvious. What will Salamander do now? Have Gower and Rue got the lizard by the tail?

Eric shook his head, dropped the paper on the settee and went to the kitchen to make himself a cup of coffee. The Salamander meeting he had attended would seem to have achieved what it set out to do: expose the fangs of Gower and Rue with their 'final' offer. It was hardly a world-shaking way of putting your house in order, nevertheless.

While the coffee was percolating he went back to the sitting-room and picked up the phone. He dialled Leonard Channing's home number. He got through right away.

'Channing.' The tone was snappish.

'You've seen the newspapers?' Eric asked.

'It's you, Ward. Yes, I've seen the reports. Trying to get maximum leverage, launching at the weekend. The open offer in the advertising section, too.'

'They mean business.'

'So do we. There's a board meeting Monday afternoon. I'll have the records of the

79

last meeting for your signature. You can make it, of course.'

Eric hesitated, thinking over his week's programme. 'I'll be there.'

'It should be an interesting meeting.'

It should indeed, Eric thought: the battle was hotting up.

★   ★   ★

The air of tension was palpable in Paul Everett's office on Monday afternoon. That he disliked Hugh Nelson was obvious from the first meeting; that he now felt they had waited too long already by making the shares plus cash offer to the wavering shareholders hardly needed emphasizing. But he emphasized it.

'It was a bloody weak response. It gained us nothing.'

'It brought some of the rats out of the holes,' Nelson observed calmly. 'The small shareholders, the nervous guys who have no stomach for the fight.'

Everett glared at Leonard Channing. 'Well, Channing, what do you have to say about it? We took a bloody hammering in the press over the weekend—they all see us as lying on our backs getting raped.'

Leonard Channing smiled thinly, his patrician nostrils wrinkling in disdain for the press. 'Their view of our position is somewhat melodramatic. It's not as weak as they make out. As Nelson says, what's happened now is that the decks have been cleared for action. What is important is that we can now set our sights on the decision makers, the institutional investors. We must target them, if we are to overcome the new Gower-Rue offer.'

'Target them with what? A new package? What can we afford by way of a counter bid?'

Leonard Channing pursed his lips. 'I'm afraid I have to advise that the financial package I put together for you, in making the last offer of shares plus cash, has taken Salamander very near the limit. The bonds issue hasn't been quite as successful as we might have hoped; we're still afloat, but any extension of the package will cause some listing of the boat—'

'Very colourful,' Everett sneered, 'but where does that leave us?'

Hugh Nelson straightened in his chair. 'Where you've always been since you came to London, Everett: in trouble. The point is, what to do about it?'

Everett drew his brows together darkly, and inspected the arbitrageur. Anger stained his eyes, but he kept it under control. After a long pause, he said in an icy voice, 'Okay, what *do* we do about it?'

Nelson smiled. 'How come you called your company *Salamander*?'

Everett, slightly taken aback, shrugged. 'Not my choice. Originally, before I took over, they had some product or other . . . but what the hell's the importance of that now, anyway?'

'Do you know about the salamander?' Nelson persisted. 'Ward, do *you* know what the salamander is?'

Eric raised his head. 'A kind of lizard, of a fabulous kind.'

'And the fable?'

'It lived in fire.'

Nelson glanced towards Paul Everett. 'The kind of fire you're living in right now, seems to me.' He turned back to Eric. 'You'll probably be able to tell us, then, how the salamander managed to live in the fire.'

Eric shrugged, not understanding the point Nelson was leading up to. 'The fable is that the salamander quenched the fire by the chill of its own body.'

'That's right.' Nelson smiled. 'The salamander chill. I think there's something we can learn from that.'

'I'm damned if I can see what,' Everett said quietly after a short pause, but there was something in his eyes and manner which led Eric to believe the man was not entirely truthful. He watched while Nelson stared at Everett: their glances locked, and they seemed to be reaching some silent agreement, wordless, but binding in understanding.

'As I understand what you're getting at,' Leonard Channing said thoughtfully, 'you're suggesting that we fight off Gower and Rue by using our own internal strengths.'

'Something like that,' Nelson replied in an offhand manner.

'So you aren't going to propose a restructured financial package?' Eric asked.

'Channing's already told us that ain't on.' Confidently, Nelson went on, 'I told you last time that Salamander was already past the point where it could fight in its own defensive trench. We've got to get out there and grab the bastards by the throat. We've got to *attack*—'

'And use the strengths we have,' Everett added quietly.

'Which are?' Channing's question hung in the air for several seconds. Nelson looked at him, but made no reply; a small smile touched his mouth as Everett also said nothing. Eric sat back, waiting. At last Everett rose abruptly, announced a break and left the room. The tension eased, as Nelson took out a pack of cigarettes and lit one. He gestured with the cigarette towards Eric. 'Your wife . . . she owns Morcomb Estates, doesn't she?'

'That's right.'

'Interesting company. Good financial profile. There's a whisper doing the rounds that they'll be buying in something soon.'

'There are always whispers,' Eric replied noncommittally.

Nelson laughed, and dragged on his cigarette. 'Don't worry, I'm not thinking of entering the lists. That kind of business is too small and too long-term in its projected benefits for a guy like me. I like to be in and out quickly—with no long-term commitments. But good luck with it . . . I hear they're a firm with prospects.'

Eric made no response. He was disturbed, nevertheless, that Anne's plans with regard to Roger Graham, Ltd were known, and among entrepreneurs in the City, at that. It was something he'd need to warn her about.

Nelson was watching him; it was possible his thoughts were in his face, for Nelson was smiling again. 'It's about *networks*, Ward. The kind of business I'm in, information comes in from all sorts of sources. And you pick it up from wherever you can, even if it seems worthless. You never know when it will come in useful . . .' Leonard Channing touched Eric's arm. 'The records of the last meeting. You can sign them now.'

There were two single sheets of paper. The account of the meeting, and the decisions taken, was brief. 'It's a bit vague,' Eric suggested.

'It's just for the Martin and Channing board,' Channing advised. 'It'll be all they need. I'll append details of the bond issues

84

and the total financial package negotiated for Everett later.'

Something still prickled at the back of Eric's mind, but the notes seemed innocuous enough. He placed his signature to the record and handed the papers back to Channing who put them away in his briefcase.

The door opened and Paul Everett came back into the room. He gave no reason for his abrupt withdrawal and he scowled as he saw that Nelson was smoking, but he made no comment. 'Right. Let's get on with it. Nelson, you're calling the play. What do you propose?'

Nelson nodded. 'Okay. Gower and Rue have now shown the colour of their money. They've made a "final" offer for the Salamander shares. It's their response to our earlier counter-offer of a mix of shares and cash—which shook out the nervous guys in the system. The decks are now clear.'

'We would not advise a better offer,' Channing intervened. 'So you're suggesting a restructured one?'

Nelson shook his head. 'No. I propose that we stand pat with the existing offer.'

There was a short silence. Eric leaned forward, interested. 'But that can't match the new bid from Gower and Rue. Salamander shares will trade away and the battle will be over for control.'

'No.' Paul Everett's tone was harsh. He

kept his eyes fixed on Hugh Nelson. 'I know what Nelson's driving at. We stand with the present offer—which is one we can afford . . . and we impose the salamander chill.'

'I don't understand—' Eric said, but Everett ignored him.

'I've made a few calls,' Everett said to Nelson. 'I think it could be on.'

Nelson stubbed out his cigarette. 'I thought it might be. All right, Channing, I'd better spell it out because your firm is going to be central to the strategy. We've flushed out Gower-Rue's final bid. If we assume it *is* final, we know that they're as fully stretched as they can afford. We also know that, like us, they'll be financing their bid by a junk bond issue. Fine. Now we know our bid can't match theirs, so what we do is make it too expensive for them to play the game.'

'And how do we do that?'

'We set up a fan club,' Nelson said flatly.

There was a short silence. The muted roar of the London streets came through as a confused murmur of sound in the boardroom; the tick of the moving minute hand on the wall clock was loud.

'You propose to sharply enhance the share value of Salamander,' Channing observed.

'That's right.'

'And the fan club—'

'We're going to put the chill on our friends,' Everett intervened coldly. 'There are

86

a number of people who owe us, and there are others who over the years have been dependent upon Salamander. They're still tied to us in a number of ways: contracts, products, share dealings, information trade-offs. I'll be giving you a list, Channing. It'll be your business to set up the deals with them. The fan club will consist of a number of rich clients, and a series of financial institutions who'll be persuaded to make some fairly large purchases of Salamander shares.'

'*Persuaded?*'

'We'll have to offer them certain guarantees, of course.'

'Such as?'

'Repurchase in due course, at a profit to them.'

'It's a high risk strategy, Nelson.'

'It's a high risk business,' Everett said sharply. 'And we're in a corner. Thing is—can you do it, Channing?'

Leonard Channing made a steeple of his fingers and inspected it thoughtfully. He considered the matter for a short while. 'If they do buy in, the share price will accelerate and Gower-Rue will be frozen out. But the repurchase condition could be disastrous for Salamander—'

'As a merchant banker, what's your prediction for this summer's market?' Nelson asked in a bland voice.

Channing grimaced, wriggled in his chair. 'That's always a problem . . . but . . . the signs are the market will rise. But it's a gamble.'

'Life is a gamble,' Everett snapped, 'and Salamander's life is on the line.'

Eric had been silent, listening hard. But it was time to step in: if Leonard Channing had meant what he said, Eric needed to intervene. 'You're taking another chance,' he said abruptly.

Their eyes turned to him. 'Talk to me,' Everett demanded.

'There are legal traps. The City Code. You can't buy in your own shares to inflate the price artificially.'

'But we're not doing that,' Everett countered. 'Our *friends* will buy in—'

'Against guaranteed purchase.'

'It's legal,' Nelson insisted.

Eric looked at him. 'There's another way of putting it. It's not *illegal*, but it's getting borderline.'

'And that's your function,' Channing said. 'Keep us the right side of the line. You have to agree, we'd be within the law?'

Eric hesitated. 'Provided the guarantees are properly drawn . . .'

'They'll be properly drawn,' Everett announced crisply. 'Right. Channing, you'll get the list this afternoon.'

'One further point,' Eric interrupted.

'These buyers . . . will any of them take more than a five per cent stake?'

Everett eyed him carefully. 'It's possible.'

'Then they'll have to be declared.'

'Some of them . . . won't like that.'

'It's got to be done—otherwise it's illegal,' Eric insisted. 'I'm aware secrecy is essential in this game; but either you keep their shareholdings below a five per cent stake or they have to be disclosed.'

'If their purchases come into the open,' Nelson said, 'the market will know what's happening and our strategy will be blown. This has to work fast and quietly, to be effective. So . . . okay . . . nothing above a five per cent stake to anyone.'

'Agreed,' Everett growled, glaring sourly at Eric. 'Now there's one favour additionally that can be called in. Garden City Enterprises—Jack Johnson. He owes me. I want his arm twisted, to support this deal.'

'That'll be Ward's task, I think,' Channing said sweetly. 'So we'll be certain that the . . . arm twisting, as you put it, is undertaken in a legal fashion.'

2

Below the summit of the hill was Temple Wood, aisles of ash and beech with the bracken thrusting dense between. As Eric walked through, climbing the hill, there were stirrings in the undergrowth, startled birds, the white scut of a rabbit. The sun was high, but the day was cool with an east wind coming in from the coast, bringing with it the hint of brine, even this far inland.

Anne had arrived the previous evening but had had to go across to Chollerford, so Eric had seen little of her. She had managed to tell him that the Grahams were expected for the weekend, as part of the general softening-up process as she put it, but she'd be back before they started to arrive. Everything was in hand, in any case. So Eric's morning was free, and he chose to take some exercise, get the morning air in his lungs on the fell above Sedleigh, and think things through about Salamander.

He came out of the wood and took the last short, steep climb to the top of the rise. The crags loomed up there, rocky outcrops grey with lichen and moss; seated there he could see the spread of Sedleigh below him, the farmlands spreading north towards the hogsback of Cheviot, hazy in the morning sun, and to the east there was the distant glint of the sea. He sat back, leaning against the rough crag and thought again about the Salamander business.

His instincts told him there was something wrong about the whole affair. He didn't trust Leonard Channing, to begin with, and while he didn't quite understand what the financiers were up to, somewhere in the assumptions there was a flaw. He could appreciate that if the 'fan club' were persuaded to buy into Salamander the share price would rise and Gower and Rue would be frozen out; the guaranteed repurchase was another matter. Setting aside the legalities of it all, doubtful as they were, and assuming the market would still rise thereafter, he would have thought that the repurchase would financially cripple Salamander in any event—supported by junk bonds or not.

Clearly, he didn't know the complete picture—but was that merely his lack of understanding, or was it a mere omission on the part of Everett, Nelson and Channing?

There was another, more unsettling explanation: he was being kept in the dark deliberately.

He had tried to draw Channing after the meeting but the man had been evasive. He'd insisted it could all come right, as Nelson had said, *assuming* the market kept moving upwards. 'And let's get one thing clear, dear boy,' Channing had assured him with a wolfish smile, 'either way, Martin and Channing doesn't lose. Should Salamander go under, we still get our fees; on the other hand, if the chill works we get our fees and an enhanced reputation for doing the business so skilfully behind the scenes.'

It was an assurance that nevertheless left Eric feeling concerned: he would have preferred a situation in which he felt more in control.

*   *   *

Anne returned from Chollerford in the late afternoon. Eric met her on the front steps and led her out to the terrace, where drinks were ready for them.

Anne sprawled in her chair, put her head back, and took a long pull at her gin and tonic. 'God, I needed that. It's been a long day. Bloody tenant farmers!'

'You've got a manager. Why do you bother?'

'Ah, it's so different from the rest of Morcomb Estates business. And it gets me out into the countryside—away from the financial wheeling and dealing.'

'There'll be a bit of that this weekend,' Eric reminded her.

She glanced at her watch and took another gulp at her drink. 'That's right. I hadn't forgotten and time's getting a bit tight. I haven't checked on the arrangements—'

'I have.' Eric paused. 'There'll be one less adversary to worry about.'

'Yes?'

'Chris Graham won't be attending the weekend entertainment. He's otherwise engaged, it seems.'

Anne pulled a face. 'That's no great loss.

He's no interest in the negotiations, anyway.'

'Not quite true. He wants as much money out of it as he can get.'

'Just as well he's out of the way, then. To our advantage.'

'To our disadvantage, in my view,' Eric disagreed. 'He's a thorn to his father and brother—he wants something different from them and isn't concerned with the future of the company. To that extent he divides the ranks on the Graham side, and they can't concentrate on a united front in argument. He's a weak link for them.'

'Do you think he's been deliberately kept out of the way?' Anne asked.

Eric shook his head. 'No, the impression I got when Roger Graham rang was that the old man was niggled by Chris's backing off at the last minute.' He hesitated. 'By the way, I don't think I told you that your talks with the Grahams are a matter of gossip in the City.'

Anne stared at him in surprise. 'You can't be serious.'

'I was asked about it in London.'

'But it's small beer! By City standards, that is.'

'Look after the pennies . . . Don't get me wrong, Graham's is an unquoted company, but people are watching Morcomb Estates, noting what you're up to. Interesting, isn't it?'

'Very,' Anne said thoughtfully. 'But

equally of interest is, who's blown the whistle?'

'I thought you'd wonder that.' Eric sipped his brandy and soda. 'It might be worth finding out what young Chris Graham's been up to with his time recently.'

'You think he's been shopping around for an offer better than the one we've come up with? He can't *do* that!'

Eric shrugged. 'You have an agreement with them that they'll talk to no other potential purchaser until you've settled details. I'm pretty sure the old man and Nick Graham will stick to that . . . somehow, I don't have the same confidence in Chris Graham.'

From the look on Anne's face, he gained the impression she similarly distrusted the youngest of the Grahams.

*   *   *

Roger Graham and his son Nick arrived just before seven that evening. They were shown to their rooms and invited to join Eric and Anne in the drawing-room at eight, for pre-dinner drinks.

They came down promptly, both men wearing dark suits, Roger Graham slightly self-conscious as he looked around him. With a glass of whisky in his hand he recovered something of his natural belligerence. 'I was raised in Byker, me,' he said. 'I was always brought up to think there was something wrong, living in places like this.'

'I pounded the beat in Byker for several years,' Eric rejoined. 'But I have to admit, I'm getting used to living at Sedleigh Hall.'

'Aye, well, you know what I mean . . . Fact is, of course, I built up my business so my bairns could live in style, so it's no different, really. Copper . . . aye, I heard you was in the force in Newcastle some years back. Bad combination for the villains, I reckon, copper turned lawyer.'

'Is there anyone else joining us this evening?' Nick Graham asked.

Anne shook her head. 'Mr Edmonds will be with us in the morning for our discussions, but I thought we could treat this evening as a largely social occasion—get to know each other a bit better, you understand.'

'Aye.' Roger Graham looked a little uncomfortable. He twisted the glass in his hand, staring at the whisky. 'I reckon I have to apologize for . . . for my younger son, Mrs Ward. He was invited, I know, and it was . . . bad manners to pull out at the last minute.' His mouth twisted suddenly, as anger gripped him. 'He's old enough to have more sense! Damned infatuation! And it's not as if—'

'Chris was called away on business,' Nick Graham interposed quickly. 'He had to get down to London at short notice. Even so, it was, I agree, bad manners not to put off the . . . the business. I hope it's not put you out too much.'

'Not at all,' Anne replied smoothly. Eric looked at Roger Graham. He was glowering at his son: clearly, Nick was covering up for his brother and the old man disapproved. But it was none of their business: that was obvious from Nick's swift reaction.

Eric thought it time to change the subject. 'I see the DTI are getting a bit active again.'

'Not before time, if you ask me,' Roger Graham said, making a humphing noise to emphasize his displeasure. 'People like us up north, we keep our heads down, work hard all our lives and society and employment collapse around us, and then down there in the City there's fat cats who pick up thousands . . . millions, just by making a few phone calls.'

'Illegal calls, of course,' Eric murmured.

'I'm not up with this conversation,' Anne admitted. 'What's been happening?'

'There's been another wave of rumours,' Roger Graham advised, 'suggesting that some of the trading in recent months has been by way of insider dealing. The DTI, the press tells us, is going to launch another investigation, particularly, into the Reeves Grenham trading. It's said that a number of prominent dealers in the City have used privileged information to buy and sell shares in advance of the market.'

'I thought the City Code—'

'The City Code *is* worth the paper it's written on,' Roger Graham sneered. 'But little more. Self-regulation will never work. Can you really expect people to resist the temptation when there's so much money to be made, just by lifting the phone a few hours before you should?'

'They'll have difficulty, of course,' Eric suggested, 'pinning down the culprits, I mean. Unless they can identify the offshore bank accounts such people use, it's next to impossible to trace just where the dealings have occurred.'

Anne caught the eye of the butler at the door. 'I think,' she said, 'it's time we went in to dinner.'

★   ★   ★

The evening passed well enough. Over dinner, Roger Graham entertained them with stories of Newcastle in the 'thirties, and the war years when the shipbuilding industry was in full swing. The old man seemed fit enough, in spite of his heart attack, although Eric noticed the surreptitious way in which he managed to take his pills with a glass of wine. He gave Eric the impression of a tough, sincere character who had come up the hard way, built a business based initially upon his own graphic skills, and who did not want to see that business die. He was reluctant to see control pass to others, but he was prepared to accept it—on the best terms he could get—provided the business continued and still bore his name.

There was a similar commitment from his elder son. Nick Graham would never stand too long in his father's shadow: there was an impatience in his manner on occasions as his father talked, and Eric guessed the two men would rarely have a smoothly running relationship. They recognized each other's strengths, but had begun to pull in different directions of recent years: that much, Edmonds's market intelligence had given Morcomb Estates. But it was more personal than that also: the old man's belligerence and straight talking jarred on Nick Graham, and the son was hard put to it on occasions to take a back seat when his father held sway with opinion.

It was a social occasion, nevertheless, and Nick Graham controlled his tongue, even if he did imbibe rather freely of the brandy after dinner.

The following morning was bright. Eric was up early, and took a cup of coffee on the terrace. He heard a step behind him and turned, surprised to see Nick Graham, clear-eyed in spite of the amount he had drunk at dinner. He wore light-coloured slacks, an open-necked shirt and sweater.

'Grand morning.'

'It is,' Eric agreed. 'Breakfast—'

'Never bother with it.' Nick Graham looked around him, appreciatively. 'Like to get some exercise first thing. Thought I'd take a stroll.'

Eric hesitated. 'Do you mind if I join you?'

Nick Graham glanced at him, smiled slightly. 'It's your land.'

Eric finished his coffee and the two men left the terrace, to walk down the drive and out across the meadow, as Eric suggested. The bridle path led up through the copse of trees to the rise, and beyond that there was a track that skirted Top Farm and took them towards the first of the crags overlooking the burn and offering the spreading views above Sedleigh itself. Nick Graham walked quickly, and his breathing remained even in spite of the rising ground. He was reasonably fit, and used to walking, Eric concluded.

When they reached the crags, they paused to take in the view. The early morning mist had not yet been burned off the hills, and layers of drifting white hung in the valleys. There was a immense quiet about them, as though the morning had not yet come alive; it was broken after a little while by the vague murmur of a tractor in the distant fields.

'So what do you think, then?' It was a

demand, rather than a question.

'About what?' Eric asked.

'Our company, of course!' Nick Graham replied, almost snappishly, as though there could have been nothing else on their minds. 'Your people have had access to information, and the investigating team have been in. You must have formed some views.'

'It's not really my concern,' Eric replied.

'But Mrs Ward . . . she'll have talked it over with you. I can't believe you remain . . . entirely distant in the matter.'

'I think I could say,' Eric suggested carefully, 'that if I were involved directly, I'd be pretty happy at what's been uncovered with regard to items other than financial data. You know, the marketing, manufacturing and research and development details that your people have supplied.'

'It's a good business,' Nick Graham announced aggressively.

'No one doubts that.'

'The old man . . . he's got it wrong. But if we can pull off an agreement . . . the extra investment . . .' Nick Graham hesitated. 'We could do with some support.'

There was a short silence. 'Things don't quite work like that in our family,' Eric said coolly.

'I didn't mean . . .'

'Shall we walk?'

It had been a clumsy opening shot, and a

100

line Eric was closing down even before it got started properly.

He should have shrugged off the clumsy approach, but he found himself irritated by it: possibly it had something to do with the feeling that Nick Graham was crass enough to think he could be suborned, his support bought in by some method or other. The irritation persisted, so that by the time Jim Edmonds arrived at ten-thirty Eric suggested, to Anne's surprise, that he might take part in the proceedings.

'I thought you didn't want to get involved,' Anne said. 'I'm pleased, of course, and you're welcome to sit in—'

'That's all I want to do,' Eric insisted. 'Sit in, and listen.'

It proved to be a fascinating meeting, but for unexpected reasons. Jim Edmonds arrived in his lightweight suit and crumpled shirt, looking as though he had spent the night before working on the books. His heavy, handsome face was set; there was a weariness about his eyes and a grimness about his mouth that suggested he was not in the best of humours. Any sense of goodwill that had been developed the previous evening between Anne and the Grahams quickly evaporated when Edmonds opened the discussions. It was clear he had come ready, looking for trouble.

'I now have the team report,' he said

crisply. 'I think I should make my own position clear, as adviser to Morcomb Estates. Our approach will be that a maximum offer could be made only if full and comprehensive information is supplied.'

'That's understood—' Roger Graham began.

'Not by your people, it seems. To begin with, your profit forecast is inflated and bears little relationship to the reality disclosed by past performance.'

'Research and development costs—'

'Your sales projections are based upon hope rather than scientific evaluation of the market potential,' Edmonds interrupted sharply. 'You have made no disclosure of indemnities undertaken, and there has been no references in your papers to subsisting licence agreements. We did, in addition, ask for copies of internal management accounts so they could be studied off-site. These were not forthcoming.'

'It was an unreasonable request,' Nick Graham said angrily. 'Security—'

'Without such cooperation we cannot make an appropriate evaluation of the worth of the company,' Edmonds asserted.

There was a long silence. Roger Graham was making a fierce effort to control his temper; Nick Graham's lips were white at the edges. As for Jim Edmonds, Eric was puzzled. He had expected a smoother negotiating technique: this bull-at-a-gate approach was hardly likely to produce the atmosphere in which progress could be made. Moreover, as he stared at Edmonds Eric was left with the feeling that there was more to this than business: two spots of high colour marked Edmond's cheeks and he glared at Nick Graham in a manner that suggested positive dislike.

Anne finally broke the silence. 'I have to say,' she suggested in a mollifying tone, 'that wasn't quite how I'd seen the papers—'

'My advice—' Edmonds began harshly.

He stopped when Anne raised her hand. Eric leaned back and listened: Anne handled the situation with delicacy and admirable control. She asked Edmonds to take each of the points in turn, but persuaded him to advance them with less heat. The Grahams still wriggled, seething, but Anne kept them in check, cooling the situation, bringing the discussion to a more acceptable plane. 'Now as to the licensing agreements . . .' she said.

'A capital equipment manufacturer,' Edmonds said. 'A fourteen-month forward order book at fixed prices with a totally inadequate allowance for inflation.'

'I'll look into it,' Nick Graham said. 'Chris—'

Jim Edmonds flared. 'And there's the patent in the electronics company—a renewal of the licence must be negotiated within eight

103

months—it could cost a packet. Why wasn't it mentioned?'

'I said I'll look into it, dammit! These are oversights—'

Edmonds was difficult to control. He was edgy, unable to keep his hands still and his tone was brittle. It was as though he were under some considerable strain which made him short-tempered: his fuse remained short as the meeting wore on. When they broke up for lunch, Anne took the opportunity to have a brief conversation with him privately. Eric looked after the Grahams: they were moody and rebellious, clearly feeling they were being set up in some indefinable manner by Edmonds.

After lunch the meeting continued in an edgy, snarling, largely unproductive manner. Anne worked hard to keep things on the rails but Edmonds seemed possessed by a manic determination to score over the Grahams, and in a way that would expose their humiliations at being unable to answer his probing questions or resolve the issues he highlighted. Eric was fascinated: something was burning at the accountant, and his dislike of father and son was patent. It was surprising that it spilled over so clearly to affect his performance: he seemed incapable of separating professional and private judgments.

At five in the afternoon, Anne asked Jim

Edmonds to sum up. The man was still feverish in his speech, sharp in his attitude. It was a performance that left the Grahams drained and Anne irritated. They sat grim-faced as Edmonds came to his conclusions.

'I think Morcomb Estates should still be interested in the proposals but only on the basis of fuller and more comprehensive information being supplied. In addition, I have been able to determine that there are in fact *three* separate activities in the present firm, even though they are not designated as divisions. Only one of these makes a clear profit; it would also be of strategic importance overall if Morcomb were to offer support and buy in. The second operation breaks even, and could sensibly be retained, using as it does the raw materials developed on the computer graphics side. The third operation—the original base—closing down seems appropriate in order to obtain a reasonable return on investment.'

'Over my dead body,' Roger Graham snarled.

Eric had the feeling that even that could be one of Jim Edmonds's recommendations to Morcomb Estates.

Anne looked around at the tense faces about the table. She sighed. 'I think we'd better break there. I'm sure we've all got a lot to think about.' She glanced involuntarily at

Jim Edmonds. 'And talk about. May I suggest we relax for a couple of hours now: please take advantage of Sedleigh Hall. Then we can meet, say at six-thirty or seven for a drink, and if we treated dinner as a semi-business occasion, maybe we can go over some of the points raised by Mr Edmonds then.'

Jim Edmonds leaned forward. His jaw was tense; a muscle twitched in his cheek, and his breathing was ragged. 'Mrs Ward . . . I regret . . .'

Anne looked at him. 'What's the problem?'

'I'm afraid I can't stay for this evening's meeting.'

'But I thought we'd arranged—'

'I'm sorry,' Edmonds interrupted nervously. 'I have another engagement I can't break. It's imperative . . . I'm sorry.'

There was a short silence. Anne's feelings, were clear from her expression. She had engaged Edmonds as a consultant, he had agreed to act in the negotiations with the Grahams and now, just after he'd delivered a tough line to them he was backing lamely out of the inevitable confrontation, leaving her to face the arguments without his support and detailed knowledge. 'I'm not sure this is acceptable—'

Edmonds stood up. His face was paling, but there was a determination in his voice that brooked no argument and no discussion.

'I regret it. I'm sorry, but I'm called away.'

He hesitated, glanced around the table a little shame-facedly, then turned back to Anne. He bowed slightly, in an oddly old-fashioned gesture that perhaps underlined the shaky position he felt himself in and then abruptly turned and stalked away from the table.

'Bloody hell . . .' Roger Graham rumbled under his breath.

'Let's break now,' Anne said grimly and rose.

While the others went upstairs to their rooms, Eric followed Anne into the library. She was standing with the palms of her hands flat on the gleaming mahogany table, her head bowed. As she heard him approach, closing the door quietly behind him, she raised her head. Her eyes were blazing with anger: he had never seen her in such a rage before. 'What the hell was *that* all about?'

'Edmonds—'

'Does he really think he can get away with behaviour like that? He's getting a bloody fat fee, and he expects me just to take a slap in the face like that? What's got *into* the guy? Where's his professional integrity gone suddenly? I mean, dammit, that summing up was hardly conducive to a reasonable negotiation—half of it was ultimatum! Does he expect people to respond to *that* kind of approach? And then just to walk off into the sunset? What's got *into* the man?'

She didn't really want a reply. Eric walked across to the cabinet against the far wall, opened it and selected a whisky for her. He poured her a stiff drink and handed it to her, put one hand on her shoulder. She fought back prickling tears, and placed her head briefly on his shoulder. 'No, dammit, I don't want to act like a *woman*!'

'There was something biting at Edmonds,' Eric suggested. 'I'm not trying to excuse his behaviour, but there's been something wrong with him ever since he walked into the house this morning. He's been edgy, uncontrolled, bothered about something.'

Anne took a deep breath, recovering her temper. She eyed the glass of whisky for a moment, then took a pull at it. She gasped slightly. 'Ahh . . . I don't know. I should have nailed him there and then . . .'

'It wouldn't have done any good. He was shaky; he was determined to go. Nothing would have stopped him.'

She shook her head. 'I don't understand . . . He looked suicidal to me.'

'So what are you going to do about this evening?'

Anne shrugged. 'Fight it through. The summary Edmonds gave is a starting point. The rest of his contribution today—there's more than enough to talk about. I think my best bet is going to be to take their reactions, and just balance the arguments without going into the kind of detail that Edmonds could.'

'That sounds a sensible strategy.'

'You'll help?'

Eric hesitated. 'All I can.'

'It won't get resolved this weekend.'

'You'll have your work cut out just stopping the Grahams damaging the furniture as they bounce off the walls.'

'Or off each other.' They were both grinning, suddenly, conspiratorially, laughing after the tension of the last few minutes. 'They're hardly a negotiating *team*, are they?'

'Imagine what it would have been like if Chris Graham had been here, instead of off on his London jaunt, or wherever he is.'

'We'd never have reached a vote. There would have been four different resolutions.'

'All contradictory.'

'What the hell are we laughing at?' Anne demanded. 'This is serious business!'

Eric reached out for her and drew her close to him. 'No. It's a good marriage.'

He gave her a long, affectionate hug; she returned it. She was having a tough time, but she was showing her mettle. He felt a considerable sense of pride in the way she was handling things. She didn't need him, but if she thought she did, he'd be there. The thought of Edmonds crossed his mind. The man's behaviour had been distinctly odd—it was as though he was being swept along by some emotional crisis over which he had no control. What had Anne said about him . . . he looked almost suicidal when he left?

Eric would have said . . . *murderous.*

3

He parked the car some two hundred yards from the mews flats. He˙switched off the lights and sat in the darkness for a little while. There was a thunder in his chest, and he became aware that his hands were trembling. Lack of control. That was bad. What he needed now was every ounce of control he could get: he mustn't let this thing get to him too badly. Stay cool; think; calm down; stop trembling.

He took a few deep breaths and waited. Gradually the tension eased and his heart rate slowed. He peered up at the sky: it was a dull night, dry, no moon. He got out of the car and locked it.

He wore a dark sweater and slacks; his trainers made no sound as he walked.

The streets were deserted. He avoided the pools of light that lay under the street lamps: in this area they were fashionably old-fashioned, electrified relics of the Victorian gas lamps. He saw no one; no cars passed, although there was the rumble of traffic from the main road some three hundred yards away.

A light glowed in the front entrance to the

flats. He felt in his pocket for the keys. The smaller one was for the front entrance; the Yale key gave entry to the flat itself. He waited, the thunder growing in his chest again as his blood coursed more rapidly through his veins. He cursed, willed himself to calm down. At last he moved forward, into the light of the front entrance, inserted the key and stepped swiftly through the doorway, closing the door gently behind him and immediately crossing the narrow hallway so that he was outlined only briefly in the light through the front door.

He hesitated. Think. *Think*!

The door lay ahead of him. He selected the Yale key. From his hip pocket he drew a pair of thin cotton gloves. He hesitated, looked back, and then crossed to the centre of the lobby, reached up to quickly remove the light bulb. It was hot to his fingers, a second later, as he untwisted it the hallway was plunged into darkness.

He groped his way to the door. He inserted the key: it slipped in smoothly, turning without a sound. A moment later he was inside the flat.

He stood with his back to the door. His heart was thudding again, but there was no shake in his hands: the adrenalin surge was acceptable, and necessary. He turned left, towards the kitchen area: he needed some light. He opened the door of the refrigerator and stepped back into the sitting-room. The dim light from the refrigerator ensured he collided with no furniture. He stood still, looking carefully around.

Near the fireplace, standing on a low coffee table, was a dark, heavy object. He moved forward, picked it up. Heavy, solid wood: the gleam of eyes, warrior eyes, reflected in the dim light from the kitchen.

With the heavy wooden warrior in his hand he turned, moving lightly towards the bedroom. His throat was dry, he wanted to cough, but it was essential he made no sound. The thunder was still in his chest, but there was something else there too, almost a pain, a surge of suppressed anger. It should never have come to this . . . a matter of trust . . . betrayal . . .

The door opened lightly to his touch. A small bedside light burned. She had been reading: the book was still open, lying on the bed. She still wore the glasses she used to read in bed: during the day, vanity had always dictated contact lenses, but in the bedroom, reading . . .

They gave her an oddly vulnerable appearance, as she lay there, arm flung wide beside the discarded book, hair a tangle on the pillow, the beautiful lines of her face in repose, the glasses tilted on her nose.

He took a deep breath; his hands had started to tremble again. He gritted his teeth, stepped forward hastily and stumbled.

Everything happened so quickly.

It was one of her slippers he had stepped on. He stumbled, struck the bed, she woke. It was not a slow awakening but the waking of someone disturbed, a nightmare in the darkness, a sudden starting up with a choking, pounding anxiety.

She sat up abruptly, dazed: he stood there in front of her and he had a surge of odd satisfaction that she saw him, recognized him before the heavy Maori warrior came slicing down at her head.

She had time to say nothing. The heavy wood struck her above the right eye, the blow sliding sideways towards her nose, crushing the glasses. She made a sound, an animal sound, bit it was small and muted, and then she was turning aside, slowly, wounded, dazed, only half-conscious and incapable of resistance.

She was lying on her side, moaning slightly when he knelt beside her, put his hands around her throat. The cotton gloves bit, took purchase. He squeezed.

He knelt, arching his back and he raised his head, glaring at the ceiling as he squeezed, until the blood pounded in his head and his arms ached and his fingers stiffened with the tension.

When it was over he felt exhausted, his sweater damp with the perspiration that had soaked through, his biceps trembling from the strain. But there were things to do.

He moved back into the sitting-room and began, systematically, to empty the drawers, throwing things haphazardly to the floor. Then into the second bedroom.

Then back to where she lay.

There was jewellery to be taken.

It could be thrown into the Thames, later.

4

The phone rang.

Eric turned away from the window. He had been watching the manoeuvring of a Danish freighter at its moorings on the Quayside: soon it would be slipping downriver, to take the long swing above Byker and then head out into a blustery North Sea. The river had once been heavy with international traffic: on his walls Eric had some old photographs of the Quayside at the turn of the century and earlier, the bustle of sail and steam. Now, the presence of a freighter, though not rare, was nevertheless noteworthy, though there were signs that trade was picking up somewhat.

He took up the phone. It was Anne.

'Hello, beautiful.'

'They've agreed.'

Eric smiled. 'Who's agreed to what?'

'The Grahams. A valuation meeting.'

'Surprise, surprise.'

'Maybe Edmonds's walk-out paid off after

all!'

Eric was amused by the crowing note of excitement in Anne's voice . . . but she had cause for excitement. The situation after Edmonds had left the previous weekend had been a fraught one. Before resuming the meeting the Grahams had clearly had a conversation about tactics. Disturbed by the aggressive summary provided by Edmonds, they had decided upon a strategy that would take advantage of the adviser's absence. They had turned dinner into a full-blown business discussion, battling hard, not only over the summarized position but also over some of the other minor issues he had brought to light.

They had got more than they bargained for. Anne had been a revelation to Eric. As the pressure came on, so she responded to it with the kind of dogged determination that was required by the circumstances; they had attempted to undermine her position by directing some of the argument in Eric's direction, but it had blown up in their faces. She had grabbed the problem by the throat, stating positively that the issues were nothing to do with Eric, they were her decisions and her responsibilities and if they didn't like dealing with a woman they could *take their damned company and shove it*.

The old man, particularly, had been taken aback. He had glanced, stunned, at Eric, and then to Eric's surprise he had grinned.

From then on it had got tougher, but it was a battle of wits where the protagonists respected each other.

And now, a week later, the fruits were showing.

'They want an early meeting. They've got the extra figures we asked for, and they're prepared to reconsider their position on the subsidiary contracts and divisions.'

'What about Edmonds?'

'Hah!' She sounded triumphant. 'I got him on the phone. He sounded . . . contrite. He'll be at the meeting, and has promised to give me a report on the new position figures before the meeting convenes. Tell you what, he sounded a much chastened man.'

'Wouldn't anyone be, dealing with a termagant like you?'

'This termagant is prepared to crack a bottle of champagne with an old warhorse tonight, if he can make it back to the stable.'

'I'm whinnying at the thought. But this meeting . . . you want me there?'

'It'd be nice.'

'So I can watch your triumphant business march?'

'So you can hold my hand when I get nervous.'

'That,' Eric said mockingly, 'will be the day.'

Ted Grainger had hit various problems with the Dawson marine insurance contracts, so he and Eric were forced to work together for a couple of days during the week that followed. During his absence, Eric felt, things had in fact got a bit slack in the office: twice when he had come in at nine he'd found the two girls in the outer office poring over the local newspaper, dwelling over the details of some local girl slaying, and he'd been irritated. He hadn't had time to read the newspapers for the last few days, even the financial sections to keep track of what the press was thinking of developments in the Salamander affair. The look on his face the second morning had been enough to bring a more businesslike appearance to the front office thereafter.

Leonard Channing rang him a couple of times, to tell him that there was no immediate meeting scheduled for the war cabinet but to expect an urgent call when things hotted up. Eric was forced to explain he hadn't had time to get to see Johnson, of Garden City Enterprises, with the brief he'd been given by Paul Everett, but promised to do it within the next few days.

Then, after that, there'd been the matter of his visit to the eye surgeon. He was always edgy before such a visit, and became more conscious of the vulnerability of his sight. On this occasion, he had so much on his mind he had little time to dwell on the matter before his visit.

He was able to report that he had had few problems of late. The scratchiness behind his eyes, the darting pains he had suffered from glaucoma had been largely alleviated as a result of the operation he had undergone, and he was sufficiently aware of the signals now to ensure that when the pressure did build up he could take immediate steps to relieve it with the pilocarpine.

The investigation was carried out, as usual, with little comment. The eye surgeon was a dour man, little given to conversation. The humphing sound he made at the conclusion of the inspection, however, meant that he was well satisfied at what he discovered.

'Things seem to be paddling along pretty well, Mr Ward. The vision remains impaired, of course, but there's no great sign of deterioration. The old advice stands: not too many hours poring over your dusty law books; try to avoid tension; learn to know when it's necessary to relax. And . . . keep taking the pills, as they say.'

It was the only little joke he allowed himself. As for his comment about avoiding tension, Eric thought again how little the man could appreciate the life a busy lawyer led: tension was inevitable, and the more so when one had to deal with people like Leonard

Channing.

The meeting arranged with the Grahams to take the matter of the acquisition further had been fixed for the Newcastle offices of Morcomb Enterprises. Anne had purchased a small block of offices in Jesmond, near the Dene, so that employees could have the opportunity to take their lunch breaks among the green and gold and copper reds of the trees that flanked the steep sides of the dene, above the stream. The boardroom on the third floor had been furnished elegantly but discreetly; Anne held the view that a working room should also be relaxing and comfortable if it were to be used to best advantage.

It was there that she held the briefing meeting before the arrival of the Grahams.

Jim Edmonds did not look well. There was a bluish tinge under his eyes and his cheeks seemed hollow, his skin dry, his colour pale. Clearly, he had not been sleeping well and although he was not overcome by the kind of nervous tension that had racked him on the last occasion they had met, he had still not recovered to present the kind of confident exterior he had shown some weeks earlier. Nevertheless, he had been working on the papers provided by the Grahams, and he was now able to take Anne through the salient points as Eric listened.

'Clearly, the aim of Morcomb Estates must be to purchase the income-generating

119

capacity of the business. There should be the minimum of unwanted assets; we don't want to get involved in any company peripheral activity.'

'I think the Grahams got your message last time at Sedleigh Hall, before you left,' Anne said. 'They didn't like it, but in the end they took it.'

'Will Roger Graham accept the need to close down the loss-making activities?'

'Most reluctantly. He might want to hive it off, keep it outside the deal, try to get it up and running on his own account.'

'That would be foolish. What about the views of . . .' Edmonds hesitated, and on odd light burned in his eyes momentarily. 'What about the sons?'

Anne shrugged. 'Nick Graham seemed to me to be accepting the strength of your argument. Chris Graham . . . who knows? I gather he *will* grace us with his presence today. Whether that will help or hinder is another matter.'

'Okay, well, I guess we'll need to explore that issue. Assuming we can reach a form of agreement on that, we'll go on to the question of valuation . . .'

Eric listened while Jim Edmonds discussed the methods of financial analysis normally used for evaluating the worth of a company. He described the relative usefulness of using earnings multiples based on firms in the same industrial sector, the amount of return on capital employed in Roger Graham, Ltd, and he went into a brief discussion of discounted cashflow analysis. Eric watched him as he talked. He was concentrating hard, attempting to get across to Anne the basic analytical techniques in a way she could use in the discussion with the Grahams, explaining the figures he had produced, but high colour burned beneath his paleness and his eyes were never still, flickering, betraying a shakiness behind the surface that suggested to Eric that the man was ill. He wondered whether he was using drugs: there was something about Edmonds that was different and uncontrolled.

'One final point,' he was saying. 'The value of a business can change in six months. Timing is important. My figures are based on *now*. There are certain predictive values built in. But if you are to acquire the Grahams' company, you should do it now—to wait would change the whole picture. I think this should be made clear to them: it's decision time for everyone.'

Anne nodded, satisfied. She glanced at Eric, raising her eyebrows. He shook his head: it was her business.

'I think there's time for a quick coffee before our friends arrive,' she said with a sigh.

They sat around the table, a little distance apart from each other, each attempting to present a different image, a separate personality divorced from the common problems facing them. Roger Graham sat nearest to Anne, who took the chair. He sat squarely, thick-fingered hands spread on the table in front of him, a pugnacious set to his mouth as though he was determined to put up a fight for the principles he believed in, his firm and himself. His grey moustache seemed to bristle defiance, but Eric guessed the man had already reached compromises in his mind or he would not otherwise be here at all.

Nick Graham sat on his father's right, not too closely. He seemed more at ease, confident, in control of the situation but his snapping black eyes were still, denoting the tension that was held in check. This was an important meeting for him: his father was coming to the end of his active business life if not his dynastic ambitions, but this was Nick Graham's future. The acquisition by Morcomb Estates had to be on the right terms, obviously, but the financial injection the acquisition could provide for the research and development phase was critical and crucial to the future expansion of Nick Graham's ideas. It would also solve the matters in dispute between father and son as to which direction the company should take.

Chris Graham sat apart. It was as though he wanted to declare both his lack of interest and his disinterest. By placing himself at the far end of the boardroom table, in touch with neither side, he appeared to be suggesting he was the honest broker in this business, the compromiser, the man who would bring things together when they looked like falling apart. If that was his view of himself, it was clearly held by no one else in the room. The others saw a slim, lightweight, fair-haired dilettante whose only interest in the matter in hand was to get out of it as much as he could, without involvement.

They were very different, the two brothers, physically, emotionally, and in their needs. Eric recalled the voluptuous Miss Frain, Nick Graham's escort the evening at Perastino's: that was Nick's style, to make use of an available female and never allow women to affect his business drive. Chris would be different: business made money; money brought the soft life. Their objectives were different.

The curious thing was, all three young men in the room seemed to be studiously avoiding looking at each other. The subdued tension under which everyone laboured at this stage, prior to the opening of the meeting, was clear enough, and understandable, but Eric felt there was something else present to bring a crackle to the air. The two brothers had come in separately, had not spoken, and were avoiding each other's eyes. Jim Edmonds was half-turned in his chair, as though to avoid recognizing the presence of Chris Graham, and facing Nick Graham as he was, he kept his head down, staring at his papers, obviating the necessity to make eye contact with the elder brother.

It might have been imagination, of course, Eric thought, but he was left with the impression that all three were uncomfortable with each other. And it had nothing to do with the business on hand.

Anne opened the meeting.

'I think we've come a long way in a short time, since first we met to discuss business. The meeting at Sedleigh Hall might be seen as a breakthrough, perhaps: not the most friendly of meetings, but at least we managed to make our positions clear to each other.'

Nick Graham managed a thin, tense smile. Roger Graham made no response, staring at his thick-veined hands.

'Mr Edmonds and I have had discussions as to how we might now proceed. If we are to talk about valuation—'

Roger Graham raised his head. 'Valuation principles if you like, Mrs Ward, but remember we haven't yet agreed the make-up of the new company and its subsidiaries.'

'Certainly; the point is made and taken.

But while that has an impact upon valuation, it's also necessary to agree valuation principles before we go further—'

'In my view,' Chris Graham cut in airily, to their surprise, 'valuation is a simple matter. The company is worth the highest sum we can obtain, from any potential bidder.'

There was a short silence. Eric leaned forward. He stared at Chris Graham for a few seconds, wondering. '*Any* potential bidder?' he asked softly.

'We've approached no other firm,' Nick Graham cut in crisply. 'Not me, not my father . . . and not Chris.'

'That *is* our agreement,' Anne said, watching Eric, recalling their conversation about gossip in the City. She waited a moment, but there was no further comment from the Grahams, so she went on. 'So the first step is to consider the basis for valuation. Mr Edmonds, perhaps you could raise the options open to us?'

Eric leaned back as the discussion swayed around the principles Edmonds now expounded. He watched Chris Graham: he didn't trust the youngest of the Graham clan, and the intervention had aroused suspicions in his mind. Chris Graham had not been present at Sedleigh Hall. His absence had embarrassed his father and brother. He had been 'called away' to London on business. Could it have been *acquisition* business . . .

the young man taking it upon himself to break the agreement and try to find another bidder who might come up with more money than Morcomb Estates?

An argument had developed between Edmonds and Nick Graham. Anne was letting it run its course: she was weighing up her own advantages, to be gained from Nick Graham's loss of control. Because the dislike that had been simmering between him and Edmonds had come through to the surface: their voices had been raised and although they were arguing about the percentage asset backing and the estimated net current asset value of Roger Graham, Ltd the real needle to their passion lay elsewhere. It was possible Anne realized it, but Eric could not be certain: she was too closely involved with the basic argument itself perhaps to recognize the underlying tensions that had enhanced its bitterness.

Eric glanced down the table to Chris Graham. The man was taking no part, but he was as tightly strung as a bow also, and his eyes were glittering oddly as the two businessmen battled it out.

Anne called a halt. 'Fine, let's agree to disagree on the point. Maybe we can come back to it when we've cooled down a bit. I'd like to introduce certain other factors for valuation purposes. I'd like your views, Mr Graham, on the competition aspects we might face.'

Nick Graham hesitated, damping down fires of resentment. 'There's always the chance the competition will bring out breakthrough products—but with a sound R and D programme we can keep a good lead in the field.'

'And what if the licence deal Mr Edmonds referred to is not in fact renewable?'

'We have assurances,' Roger Graham rumbled, clenching his fist. 'I've done business with them for years; there are still some old values around; I've every confidence—'

'There are pressures we can put on,' Nick Graham interrupted testily, as though afraid his father would become anecdotal. 'We don't need to rely upon old pals' acts—they aren't reliable.'

Roger Graham's bald head went pink. Quickly, Anne went on. 'We'll need convincing in our valuation analysis that the critical source of supply remains protected, and that acquisition can lead to an improved distribution network.'

'What *you* haven't told *us*, however,' Chris Graham announced, 'is just what you're prepared to pay for a major interest in Graham's. Sure, you talk *principles*, and you talk *analysis*, but when are you going to talk about cash?'

Jim Edmonds slowly turned his head,

dragging his glance reluctantly towards the youngest Graham. He seemed to struggle to find his voice; when he spoke, it was raspingly, his dislike oddly emphasized by the reasoned response he made. 'There is a point with which I would agree here. The price must be talked of—and I hope that we can get towards an opening bid this morning. But not prematurely: it has to be based upon an understanding of the valuation principles involved.'

'You're still not saying how much!' Chris Graham taunted, sneeringly.

The rasp in Edmonds's tone became more noticeable. 'I have already given Mrs Ward my view as to the best offer that should be made—'

'Opening offer, or final?' Chris Graham snapped in derision.

Edmonds glared at the man. 'All things are negotiable. *Experienced* businessmen know that. Only idiots presume otherwise. I can't expect you to appreciate what I'm saying, however: your presence in these negotiations seems to me to be superfluous and indeed, an irritant to any sensible discussion on a business basis.'

'You think you can talk to me like that?' Chris Graham coloured, half-rising in his chair, his fingers jerking spasmodically as though he wished to have them around Jim Edmonds's throat. 'A bloody paid lackey, a non-achiever in the real world, business or bed, I guess, forced to *advise* others rather than do it himself! The only irritant here is you, my friend—start talking to me like that when you prove yourself to be a man, the kind to hold on to a women even, and then—'

'*Chris!*' Nick Graham's voice was like a whipcrack. 'Siddown, and shut up. *Now!*' His face was white with anger and his fists were clenched. There was something of his father in him suddenly: the passion, the anger and the belligerence that made him look as though he wanted to snap his younger brother in two. 'You've said enough. It's finished. Now leave it, and let's get back to business.'

Anne was shaken. She looked to Eric; he smiled slightly, nodded. She took a deep breath. 'All right, time to cool down. A ten-minute break, perhaps, and coffee?'

It was a welcome suggestion.

The Grahams filed out, heading for the executive washroom, no doubt to make their way to the private room set aside for their use; thereafter, to hammer at each other the need to maintain a concerted front. Edmonds gathered up his papers moodily and marched out, heading for the other negotiating room earmarked for himself, Eric and Anne.

Left together in the boardroom, Anne and Eric stared at each other. Anne let out a whoofing sound. 'Just what was *that* all about?'

'Not the acquisition, I suspect.' Eric shook his head. 'They're like scorpions waving their tails at each other every time they look across the table. For some reason, there's no love lost between Edmonds and the Grahams.'

'It makes me wonder,' Anne said slowly, 'whether we should continue to use Edmonds, if this is the effect it has.'

'He has the skills, and I think he's giving you sound advice.'

'But like you said . . . scorpions.'

The door opened and the two girls came in with the trays of coffee and biscuits. Eric took Anne's hand. 'Come on, let's get some air for a few minutes.'

They walked out of the boardroom and down the corridor. At the end of the corridor there was an emergency exit; it led out to a small terrace that overlooked the car park at the side of the office block, and beyond that, Jesmond Dene.

There was a light breeze blowing from the west. It brought with it the sounds of the city, and across from Jarrow Slakes the sound of a tug siren.

'Is that a police car down there?' Anne asked.

Eric looked down to the car park. The car was stationed near the entrance to the park; a uniformed constable was behind the wheel, his arm showing through the side window as he leaned, waiting.

'They must be in this building, somewhere,' Anne suggested.

Eric frowned. Anne led the way back towards the boardroom after a few minutes and he followed; as she entered he hung back, however, allowing the remainder of the group to file in, stragglingly. Eric turned back, walked towards the lift.

Someone was coming up.

He waited.

The lift doors soughed open. A slightly flustered receptionist stood there, about to come out. When she saw Eric, relief flooded into her eyes. 'Ah, Mr Ward, this gentleman—'

Eric knew him, slightly. He was some years younger than Eric, but he had a sound reputation: he had appeared in a number of prosecutions in the Newcastle courts.

Detective-Inspector Lyle: an able man with a solid record. He didn't get sent out on trivial matters.

'Hello, Lyle.'

'Mr Ward,' Lyle acknowledged, somewhat warily.

'Business?'

'That's right.' Lyle's glance slipped past Eric towards the boardroom. 'You've got a meeting.'

'Important one.'

'I'm sorry about that.' He began to walk along the corridor. The receptionist faded into the background, as Eric walked with the detective-inspector.

'You want to see someone in the meeting? As I say, it's an important—'

'Do you think you could ask Mr Edmonds to come out? I don't want a fuss made,' Lyle said almost apologetically. 'He *is* in the meeting, I understand.'

'That's so,' Eric replied. 'I . . . I can ask him.' He hesitated, wanting to ask, but knowing he would get no satisfactory reply. Then he nodded, turned, went back to the boardroom. He caught Anne's eye, seated at the head of the table. 'Excuse me . . . Mr Edmonds, would you mind stepping outside for a moment? You're . . . wanted . . .'

Edmonds looked up. He stared at Eric without comprehension, and then slowly what colour remained in his hollow cheeks faded. He rose and walked out, his awkward, shambling gait suddenly vulnerable.

He did not close the door behind him. Detective-Inspector Lyle met him in the corridor; Eric saw him put his hand on Edmonds's wrist, before Eric closed the door and turned to face the room again.

Anne saw with a worried frown on her face, feeling the tension that had suddenly arisen in the silence. Only Roger Graham seemed unaffected. The two younger Grahams were staring at each other. Their glances were stony.

They seemed to know why Edmonds had left the room.

CHAPTER THREE

1

'Murder?'

Sunlight spilled across the broad steps at the main entrance to the hallway at Sedleigh Hall. Anne was dressed for riding; when she had heard Eric's car in the drive she had waited, sitting hugging her knees on the steps, leaning against the stone balustrade. Eric put down his briefcase, leaned over and kissed her in greeting, then sat down beside her. Shock still registered on her face.

'But I can't believe it!'

'It was on the car radio now, as I was driving up from Newcastle,' Eric confirmed. 'Jim Edmonds has been formally arrested, and it is expected that charges will be laid against him regarding the murder of Karen O'Neill.'

'But she was his fiancée!'

'So he told us,' Eric nodded.

'What's that supposed to mean?' Anne demanded.

'I don't really know. I suppose . . . well, Edmonds introduced her to us as his fiancée, but there was something . . . *odd* about the whole thing, don't you think? I got the impression he was absolutely obsessed with her—'

'Dotty.'

'But equally, it seemed to me she didn't exactly feel the same way about him. That night we met her—I know we were talking business and Edmonds couldn't dance attendance on her the way he might have wished—but I didn't get the impression she was one to pine away in a corner for lack of attention.'

'Chris Graham almost monopolized her for the first part of the evening.'

'And Edmonds was less than pleased. You remember how tense the atmosphere was in the car coming home? It was clear they were heading for a bust-up that night.'

Anne sighed, and shook her head. 'Even so, it's another story, talking about murder.'

'I agree.' Eric looked around him, squinting in the late afternoon sunshine. The trees on the hill were very still; there was not a hint of a breeze and above Cheviot a delicate tracery of cloud trailed pink-edged against the dark hogsback of the mountain. 'I wonder whether this had anything to do with the state he was in when he came here for the meeting with the Grahams?'

Anne stood up, frowning. 'He was certainly odd that day. Not himself.'

A high state of tension, Eric considered. The man had been shaky, short-tempered and, late in the day, seemingly seized with the determination to leave the meeting and charge off elsewhere at short notice. To London, perhaps? To quarrel with Karen O'Neill, and kill her? Eric shook his head. He linked his arm through Anne's. 'You going riding? Okay, I've got some paperwork to do before dinner, so I'll have that finished by the time you get back, and we'll have a drink on the terrace before we eat.'

'It's a date.'

As she turned to make her way towards the stables he called after her, 'You'll remember I'm off to Bristol in the morning?'

'Flying or by train?'

Eric hesitated. 'Train, I guess.'

*   *   *

It meant an overnight stay, of course, but Eric rarely flew if he could avoid it. His meeting in London at Martin and Channing's behest normally meant a flight from Newcastle Airport; he no longer suffered from the tension that had occurred when he was in the worst period with glaucoma, but he disliked the short haul business flights. Travelling over longer distances was not so bad: he felt less constrained and confined with room to stretch his legs, but the brief

135

flights within the UK meant cramped seating and poor service. So, if he could, he took the train.

He managed to do some work as he travelled to Bristol the next day, preparing for his meeting with Jack Johnson, the managing director of Garden City Enterprises. Paul Everett had given him a file on the relationship between Johnson's business and Salamander and it made interesting reading: there had been close ties between the two since long before Salamander had moved to London, and Eric could see that it would be in the interests of both parties that the Gower and Rue bid should be beaten off.

Inadvertently, Eric's thoughts strayed back to Jim Edmonds and the murder of Karen O'Neill. He had heard no details beyond the bare announcement of the arrest, and oddly enough neither he nor Anne had seen anything about the killing in the newspapers. He recalled the gossiping girls in the reception area of his office on the Quayside: clearly, they had been talking about the newspaper coverage of the killing, but he hadn't had time to read the papers and consequently had known nothing about it.

A fashion model slaying would have made news. But why was Jim Edmonds arrested? She would have known many people in London, the kind of life she led. Maybe that had been the trouble . . . Jim Edmonds had been obsessed with her, and jealousy could have led to violence.

At Temple Meads Eric left the train and hailed a taxi to take him to Johnson's office. The address given was interesting: it was certainly not a city address. The taxi took him through the town, up Park Street past the tower of the University and up over Clifton Downs. They crossed the suspension bridge that Brunel had built and then they were among cool woods and elegant houses, the university preserve and the havens of rich men from the days when wealth had poured into the city from the slave trade.

Johnson's 'office' was a sprawling mansion set back some little way from the road among groves of beech trees. Birds sang and the noises of the city were distant and muted. Eric paid off the taxi in front of the pillared main entrance. He looked about him. Johnson worked in stylish surroundings.

He told him so, when they met in the office on the first floor.

'And why not?' Johnson replied. 'The kind of business I do, most of it's over the telephone. Why commute into the city to do that? I can just as easily do my trading out here, where it's quiet, and pleasant, and just what is needed by a country boy like me.'

It was not how Eric would have described the man. He was short, well-padded with flesh around the stomach, and bucolic of complexion, but his button eyes were those of a city man, sharp, quick and restless. His movements too were nervous; he seemed unable to keep still. As Eric sat on the leather settee Johnson prowled, moving from table to desk to chair to window, restless, crackling with energy. It was the energy that would have made him a success in the world of share dealing and trading of commodities; it was the restlessness which made him come early to the point of Eric's visit.

'Let's say I'm not too happy about it all,' Johnson said, stabbing a half-chewed but unlit cigar in Eric's general direction. 'The fact is, I believe a guy should fight his own battles. And I don't like markers getting called in, not like this.'

'That's not quite how Paul Everett sees it,' Eric suggested. 'You have mutual interests—'

'Interests, yes, and more than that. We go way back, you know,' Johnson said, a hint of confidentiality creeping into his voice. 'I could tell you some things, tell you about some wheeling and dealing we did in New York ten years ago . . . But that kind of tightrope-walking when *seconds*—I mean *seconds*—counted in deciding whether you were broke or high as a kite, they're gone. I got a stable business now; it runs smoothly. I don't need to handle the kind of arbitraging pressures—'

'Salamander thought it didn't need to

either,' Eric reminded him, 'until Gower and Rue came along.'

'I'm not Salamander.'

'You're closely tied, in interests.' Eric hesitated, then leaned forward, offering the file to Johnson. 'Paul Everett suggested you might be interested in looking at this.'

Eric had read the file. It consisted of a list of contracts, share positions and active dealing situations in which Salamander and Garden City Enterprises were interested. In most of them Salamander was in a pole position, but in each case there was a significant financial commitment from Garden City Enterprises. Eric suspected some of them had been joint activities; in others, however, Johnson had probably followed a Salamander lead, trusting to Everett's renowned ability to buy—and sell—at the right time.

'So?' There was a certain belligerence in Johnson's tone.

'The Salamander view is that if the Gower and Rue bid is successful most, if not all, those positions will be at risk. There will be an asset-stripping exercise. Garden City Enterprises will be unable to off-load its dealing in a falling market. Some of your holdings could be halved; some of your portfolios virtually wiped out.'

'That's guesswork!' Johnson snapped.

'It's *Salamander* guesswork.'

'When Everett's got his back to the wall.'

Eric ignored the sneer. 'The truth can loom up pretty clearly when you're in that position.'

Johnson chewed on his cigar thoughtfully. He prowled the room like a chubby tiger, restless, nervous but dangerous. He slammed the file down on his desk, and shook his head. 'The bastard could be right, that's the problem . . . All right, so what's he want from Garden City?'

'It's quite simple,' Eric replied. 'Everett wants Salamander protected. The best protection is a rising share price, so shareholders aren't tempted by the Gower and Rue bid. The price will rise if there's some solid buying.'

Johnson glared at Eric. 'He wants me to buy Salamander shares at a time when he's facing the firing squad?'

'There will be others doing the same. That's the strategy.'

'I bet it is. Calling in the bloody markers . . . paying back old debts . . .' Johnson shook his head in anger, and prowled again. He glanced sideways at Eric, a twist of cunning in his voice. 'There's more to this, of course. How long will Salamander want me to hang on to the shares?'

'No time stipulated,' Eric said calmly. 'The . . . investment should not exceed five per cent, of course, because Salamander would

140

not wish the supportive exercise to become obvious to Gower and Rue too soon—'

'We keep our mouths shut, in other words. Well, that's sensible. But there must be some other guarantee.'

'Company law forbids a company to support its own share price—'

'Never mind all that balls. There's got to be something *else*,' Johnson insisted.

Eric hesitated. 'A guarantee of re-purchase.'

'At what price?' Johnson said quickly.

'That's something you must talk to Everett about. I imagine it will not leave you in a losing position.'

'Too bloody right,' Johnson agreed. 'A guaranteed re-purchase . . . after the smoke has cleared . . . I'd be taking a chance, Ward.'

'It's a risky business,' Eric agreed blandly.

The irony was lost on Johnson. He screwed up his button eyes, lost in calculation. Then he turned suddenly, hurled his damaged cigar at the wall and cursed. 'That Everett, he's a dodgy bastard, you know.' A fat, unpleasant chuckle rumbled in his chest. 'Calling in the markers . . . but offering a chance for a killing at the same time. A guaranteed re-purchase could leave me with a tidy profit at the end of the day . . . I always disliked those fancy-pants Gower and Rue people, too.' He shook his head admiringly. 'Paul

141

Everett . . . he always was a chancy one. You know, you wouldn't think it to look at him but he had the biggest appetite I ever came across. Not for food—for excitement and tightrope-walking. The two best for him have always been money and women. How the hell he's kept that third wife of his these last years I don't know, because he's hopped in and out of so many beds between here and New York . . . He kept a mistress in an apartment in Manhattan for years, and another in Tokyo. Those were in the fat USA years . . . I never heard what he might have had going in London, but there'll have been something. Whether his wife knows, or ever knew, who can tell? She's never raised waves, but then, why should she? Comfortable life. But Paul, he'll have had something going . . . dammit, he might even have rolled that O'Neill character a few times.'

Something cold touched the back of Eric's neck. *'O'Neill?'*

'Yeah. The woman who got put to sleep. Sounds just like Paul Everett's type.'

'Are you suggesting—'

The button eyes sparkled maliciously. 'Hey, don't get me wrong. I'm not suggesting Everett had anything to do with her being blown away. It was always going to be a chance she took, after all, girl like that!'

Eric leaned forward on the settee. 'She was a fashion model, wasn't she?'

142

The unpleasant chuckle came again; it was louder this time, and longer, and held a trace of genuine amusement, if of a mocking kind. 'Fashion model? You don't tell me you believe that kind of title, do you? Look, a ratcatcher is still a ratcatcher even if he describes himself as a rodent control officer! *Fashion model* in this context, Ward, means she was able to charge more than usual!'

'Charge?'

'This O'Neill woman was a high class whore!'

Eric leaned back, surprised. Johnson looked at him shrewdly. 'You're not going to tell me you guys up north are so innocent . . . hey, she was from up there somewhere, I hear. Did you *know* her?'

'Eh?' Eric shook his head thoughtfully. 'No. I . . . I met her once, recently.'

'And it didn't show, is that it?' Johnson sighed, clucked his tongue. 'Yeah, well, maybe you didn't know the signs. Fact is, Ward, the City is something else . . . Maybe it's the excitement and the pressure of the trading; maybe it's the kind of money that goes through a guy's hands. The thing is, there's no going back to put your slippers on at night and sit before the fire with the little woman. High pressure day . . . you need to unwind. And in my experience, all these high pressure guys are the same; they need the relief, and they find it. There are always *fashion models* available; sometimes it's safer, and in the long run cheaper, to set one up somewhere. Maybe this O'Neill girl was set up; all I know is, City talk is she was a whore. And believe me, the market for them in the City, at the right level, is big. Me, now . . . well, there was a time . . .' He grinned, wickedly. 'Truth is, my wife *scares* me—so it was Bristol, a few years back. Not that it stops me . . .'

A shadow crossed his eyes suddenly, as he became aware he was straying into confidentiality. He marched to his desk, took out another cigar from the box there, stuck one end in his mouth and chewed vigorously. He jabbed a pudgy finger in Eric's direction. 'Anyway, we're getting off the subject. We were talking about Salamander. So Everett's setting up a fan club, is that the way the wind's blowing?'

'That's the way.'

The cigar rolled from one corner of Johnson's mouth to the other in cogitation. After a short silence, the managing director of Garden City Enterprises nodded. 'Okay, you can go back to Salamander and tell them I'm prepared to talk figures and details. You can tell Everett, personally, I don't like getting my arm twisted, but I'll go along with it this time—if the deal is right. In other words . . .'

'Yes?'

'That re-purchase guarantee had better be

tight as a bloody drum.'

Not that Johnson would have much by way of a sanction if it wasn't, Eric thought, and Johnson knew it. If Salamander did renege on its agreement, financial credibility and the retention of image would probably prevent Johnson from complaining too loudly. But as Eric was learning, there could be many ways to skin financial cats, and he guessed Paul Everett and Jack Johnson had utilized most of them in the past.

★   ★   ★

Eric had booked into a hotel at St Vincent's Rocks, overlooking the gorge. It was a modest enough accommodation but it suited him, since it allowed him to take an evening walk along the Downs after dinner. He pondered over what Johnson had had to say about Karen O'Neill and life in the City. It would be an exaggeration of course, the view of a man who had been part of the scene but was now an outsider. Eric could understand how some of the City entrepreneurs might adopt the life style Johnson had described—and indeed, he could appreciate that there could be a link between edgy dealings, high pressure financial activities, and easy sex.

But what about Jim Edmonds? He said he was engaged to Karen O'Neill and that she was a fashion model. Had he really been so naïve—assuming the City gossip as retailed by Johnson was correct, or had his statement had some foundation in truth?

He stood at the edge of the Downs, looking at the dark gleam of the river far below him in the gorge and the string of lights along the suspension bridge. It all seemed such a long way from murder and financial deals . . . as did Northumberland. He turned on his heel and walked back to the hotel. Time to phone Anne before he went to bed.

When he got through, she sounded groggy.

'Ah, Eric, it's been a hard day, I went to bed early.'

He could imagine the musky smell of her, struggling through sleep, and the warmth of her body as she held him.

'Sorry to wake you. I thought I'd ring, let you know things went OK here, and I'll be back on the early train. I'll come straight up to Sedleigh—I won't go into the office—'

'*Eric.*' Her voice was suddenly sharper, as the fogs of sleep cleared. 'I don't think you'd better do that.'

'Why not?'

There was a short pause. 'Ted Grainger . . . from your office. He phoned this afternoon. He wanted to talk to you—I told him you'd be back tomorrow.'

'What's it about?'

'This Karen O'Neill thing. It's Jim

146

Edmonds.' She hesitated again. 'He's been charged with the murder. He wants you to represent him.'

2

It was a typical interview room: small, bare, a table and two chairs, grimy, pale-yellow-painted walls, obscene graffiti barely removed, depressing. Eric sat and waited, hands between his knees, fingers laced together. This put him back fifteen years and more, and the grind of the beat, the back streets of Newcastle, Byker, the West End, Saturday night violence and the snarl of dogs, late night hunting in a pack. The room smelled of urine, as they always did: he could never understand that.

The door opened behind him and he turned his head. Detective-Inspector Lyle stood there staring at him, a file clutched under his arm. His eyes were cool and his expression discouraging. 'Mr Ward,' he said.

'Detective-Inspector Lyle.'

The policeman came in soft-footed, closing the door gently behind him. He crossed the room, pulled out the chair on the other side of the plain deal table and sat down. He looked down at the file cover in front of him.

'You asked for an interview.'

'That's right. I've been asked to represent Jim Edmonds in the O'Neill case.'

'Can't help you. Not our manor.'

147

Eric nodded. 'I know that. I realize since the killing occurred in London it'll be an Old Bailey job eventually, with the arraignment down there as well. He's held there, and that's why I haven't seen him yet. But I thought it would be useful to . . . have a chat, find out what the case against him might be.'

'So go ask down in the Met.'

'I thought it might be better to ask here first.'

Lyle raised his head slowly. He looked at Eric and there were shadows of resentment in his eyes. 'I told you, not our case.'

'You made the arrest.'

'I made the collar for the Met. They shipped him down for questioning. Not our case. Can't help.'

'Or won't?'

Lyle bared his teeth thoughtfully and was silent for a little while. 'Just because you were a copper here once, it doesn't mean you can walk in at any time and ask for privilege, inside information, work the old pals act. I know you didn't ask to speak to me, but to one of your old mates; he's off shift, so I'm here. Fact is, Mr Ward, there's nothing owed to you here. You got out. Don't you realize there's even a bit of resentment scurrying around from time to time, especially when you give us the hammer in court?'

'It's my job.'

'Yes. Well . . .'

148

'And in the end we're both talking about justice.'

Lyle gave a short, barking laugh. 'That's a giggle! A lawyer, talking to a copper about justice? The way you guys swing things in the courtroom—when we *know* a guy is guilty?'

'And do you know Edmonds is guilty?'

Lyle shook his head. 'This is a bad one, Mr Ward. I'd walk away from it if I were you.'

'What's the story against him?'

Lyle was silent again. He stared at Eric, weighing him up, and he smiled slightly, an unpleasant twist at the corner of his mouth. 'I told you . . . it's not our case. But, I suppose, if you want the bare facts there's no reason why you can't have them. You are *representing* him, after all, and we don't want to obstruct *justice*. All right, it's like this. She was hammered, and the guy who hit her didn't like her, believe me. I seen the photographs.'

'The weapon?'

Lyle smiled again. 'A blunt instrument. But that didn't kill her. Edmonds hit her, laid her half-unconscious, forensic think. Then he just wrapped his hands around her neck, and squeezed. I tell you, he *really* didn't like that girl!'

'Strangulation . . .'

'That's it. And we can link Edmonds with the flat. We can prove he was there. We can show motive. And there's a print on the . . . blunt instrument. Open, as they say, and

149

shut. So don't go briefing any expensive silks, Mr Ward: it'll be a waste of time. Now, I don't think I can help you any more, so—'

'Just one more thing, Detective-Inspector,' Eric said.

Lyle paused, half-risen from his chair. 'Yes?'

'What do you know about Karen O'Neill?'

Lyle hesitated, and then the smile came again, more broadly, wordly-wise. 'About Karen O'Neill—a bloody sight more, apparently, than Mr James Innocent Edmonds!'

*　　　*　　　*

It was a further twenty-four hours before Eric was able to manage an interview with his new client. When he'd spoken to Ted Grainger to hear that Edmonds had been taken to London and had asked for Eric Ward to represent him, he had agreed to accept the situation with reluctance. Grainger had already taken the necessary preliminary steps, assuming that since Eric knew the man he would want to represent him. Eric had mixed feelings about it, however: the case had unpleasant overtones, he did not particularly care for Edmonds, and he was already heavily embroiled in other matters, not least the Salamander business. There was also the fact that if Edmonds was now unable to assist in

150

the matter of the Graham acquisition, Eric had the feeling he might have to spend rather more time assisting Anne than he had bargained for.

When he did finally get down to London to meet Jim Edmonds he was somewhat surprised to see the change in the man. The last occasion they had met there had still been signs of tension—a different tension from that displayed at Sedleigh Hall, but still there. Now, the man seemed calm: it was as though events had been taken out of his hands, he was no longer in control of his circumstances, and he was passive, prepared to accept what came to him. But a light had died in him, in addition: the drive and thrust he had displayed in the Graham negotiations were lacking. He was pale, and looked tired. He was a man prepared to give up, to surrender.

'So,' Eric said heavily. 'Where do we start?'

Edmonds shrugged, almost indifferently.

'*Did* you kill her?'

The eyes flickered up sharply, a quick gleam of anger directed at Eric. It died, and Edmonds shook his head. 'They say I did. It's not true.'

'They also say they can prove it.'

Edmonds was silent, staring at the table in front of him. He shrugged. 'Maybe they can.'

'What the hell's *that* supposed to mean?'

'You can prove all sorts of things . . . to yourself, for instance. That a woman

151

is—what she isn't. That she loves you. But then . . . the reality . . .'

'What *was* the reality?'

Edmonds took a long breath. He looked at his hands, inspected them, shaking his head slightly. 'The reality . . . ? Possessiveness, on my part, I suppose. On hers . . . I don't know. Indifference, in the end.'

'When she died?'

'I wouldn't know.'

'So what proof do they have? You'll have to tell me what happened, Edmonds.'

'What happened?' Edmonds seemed dazed for a moment, staring at Eric in a vague imcomprehension. 'But that's the point— what *did* happen?'

Eric had the feeling they were talking about different things: perhaps the way forward was to draw Edmonds out by concentrating on what Edmonds was concerned with. 'When did you first meet her?' Eric asked.

Edmonds frowned, contemplating a past that must now seem distant and hazy and uncertain. 'It was about two years ago. I'd been to the States, came back to Newcastle, we met at this party . . . I fell for her almost as soon as I saw her, and I thought she . . .' He shook his head. 'She was kind of at a loose end. She was thinking about going to London . . . she told me opportunities would be better there.'

'Was she working as a model in

Newcastle?'

'In a small way, I guess. I went back to the States, we wrote, she came out for a few weeks and I asked her to marry me.' He chewed at his lip, thoughtfully. 'That was a good time.'

'When did things change?'

'Change?' For a moment there was a resentment in his tone, as though he was going to deny there had been a change. The flare died, and he shrugged. 'Not long after she went to London, if I'm honest about it. She rarely wrote, said she was busy, seemed reluctant to meet me in London when I returned from the States at odd times. Then, when Mrs Ward came up with the offer, I saw it as a chance to get back for a solid period and persuade Karen to marry me.' He hesitated. 'Karen . . .' The name tasted unfamiliar on his lips: he tested the sound and it was the name of a stranger, someone he had never really known.

'Things weren't right between you at Perastino's,' Eric suggested.

Edmonds grunted. 'Before that. I asked her to come up to meet Mrs Ward: it was important to me. I suppose I wanted to tie her in with my career, my future back here in the UK. She was reluctant, but I thought I'd persuaded her. Then she called it off at the last moment, and I thought that was bad. More than that . . .' He frowned. 'I suppose

153

it made me insecure. I began to realize I was
going to have to struggle to keep her. If I'd
ever had her . . .'

'How do you mean?'

His glance was vague. 'I'm not sure now,
what she wanted. I thought . . . well, I don't
know now. Perhaps she saw something . . .
glamorous in the kind of work I was doing,
the travel, the high pressure . . . But once she
moved to London, I guess she met other
people . . . and I was small beer . . .'

Or, if she was what Johnson had suggested,
a better opportunity had come along, Eric
thought to himself. 'Did you quarrel after the
evening at Perastino's?'

Edmonds was silent for a few moments. He
shrugged. 'I don't know that you'd call it a
quarrel. I got .. upset. She was different.
Cooler; not prepared to talk to me. So I
decided to have it out with her. We discussed
it. We . . . worked it out.'

He was lying. Eric recalled the anxious
prowling at Perastino's, the jealousy, the
tension in the car on the return home. The
two had been set for a quarrel that evening,
and Edmonds was lying now. Eric let it pass
for the moment.

'So what happened after that?'

'Nothing.'

'What do you mean?'

'I didn't see her again.'

'You mean the engagement was broken

154

off?'

'Yes. No . . . not exactly.' Edmonds appeared confused. 'She said she thought it best we let things slide for a while . . . she didn't want to be tied down. I argued a bit, but she was determined . . . a strong-minded woman.'

'But you didn't quarrel?'

'It was a . . . a rational discussion,' Edmonds said slowly, like an actor rehearsing his lines.

'You agreed to part?'

'More or less.'

'So what were you so disturbed about at Sedleigh Hall?'

'Disturbed?'

Grimly, Eric said, 'Don't play the fool with me, Edmonds. You were like a cat on hot bricks that day. You were committed to our meeting and yet you behaved as though you didn't want to be there. You were impatient to get the meeting over; you wanted to be away; you tried to muscle the Grahams into submission by an all-out attack, and when it didn't work you just backed off, said you had to be elsewhere, and you shot off like a crazed rabbit. You weren't *concentrating* on the Graham acquisition, your mind was elsewhere. So what *was* bothering you? It was something to do with Karen O'Neill, wasn't it? You were obsessed with her; she wanted to finish with you; you were beside yourself with

155

anxiety—and now you tell me it had been settled *rationally*? How rational was the solution, in fact? *Did* you beat her? *Did* you strangle her? Or did you just *want* to?'

'It wasn't like that! I was in love with her and—'

'*And she was a whore!*'

The chair went over with a crash as Edmonds lurched to his feet. Anger twisted his mouth; his eyes were wild, glaring at Eric and his hands reached out, fingers crooked. 'That's not true!' he snarled.

Still seated, Eric looked up at him calmly. 'The story I hear is different . . . and maybe you heard it too. It's what the police will push as a line. They'll say she was a high class whore. You loved her; you found out; you killed her. The motive was jealousy. That's what I am pretty certain they'll say. But I understand they have more.'

He paused, and Edmonds sat down slowly, a pulse beating strongly in his throat. He did not look at Eric.

'They say they have motive,' Eric went on. 'And they also say they can link you to the flat she lived in: opportunity. The story is they can also tie you in with the actual murder. Edmonds, I can't do a damn thing to help you unless you are honest with me. You *did* quarrel with Karen O'Neill, and any competent counsel will have it out of you in the witness-box in ten seconds flat. What you

156

now *have* to tell me is what happened between you after that—and I have to know *how* the police can tie you in with that flat, and the murder.'

'I didn't kill her.'

'Then tell me your side of it. *All* of it.'

Edmonds nodded slowly, put his hand up to his neck, touched the pulse there as though he wanted to still its tremor. He shook his head; nodded; shook his head in a slow, mechanical movement as though he was trying to clear his head of the fantasies that surrounded him.

'It's true, we did quarrel. It was a shouting match, that night we got back to my flat in Newcastle. I was angry about the way she seemed to have changed, and she told me she'd only come back to tell me it was over and done with between us. I was mad as hell, and, well, she was a . . . a passionate woman, Mr Ward. In a funny way the argument excited us both . . . in the middle of it I grabbed her, shook her, there was more violence in me than I knew, and suddenly the anger was excitement and we were making love . . . and for a few hours it seemed all right again . . .'

He paused, and Eric watched him carefully. He had the feeling the man was now telling the truth.

'I woke in the early hours. She was lying there. I loved her, and we'd just made love, but I knew that once she was back in London . . . I was angry, and bitter, and I wanted to know *why* . . . I rose and went to the sitting-room. I found her handbag; I went through it. There were things there . . . I found a set of keys . . .'

'You took them?'

Edmonds nodded. 'She had two sets. One set was attached to her car keys; the other lot on a general bunch. I left the ones on the car keys tab: I guessed they'd be the ones she'd normally use, keep the others as spares. I just slipped two keys off.'

'How did you know what they were?'

'I guessed . . . but one was obviously a door key—a Yale—and the other was one of those flat things you often see used for external door locks in shared buildings.'

'What did you do then?'

Edmonds shrugged. 'Nothing, really. I stewed over things for days. After she went back she didn't contact me. I knew it was finished. I got very angry over it: got drunk a few times. And that weekend at Sedleigh . . . I'd made inquiries, you see. Checked phone books—no luck. So then I tried an inquiry agent . . .'

Eric groaned inwardly. He could see the police case building up inexorably. The inquiry agent would be one of their witnesses: he could understand Lyle's confidence now.

'The address was a smart one. Mews flat,

fashionable. How could she afford that? It gnawed at me. I had to find out. I decided that weekend, I couldn't wait any longer. You were right about Sedleigh Hall . . . but I was beside myself.'

'You went down to London, to find her?' Eric asked quietly.

Edmonds nodded.

'You found the flat. And the keys . . .'

'They fitted.'

Eric sighed. 'And you went in.'

It had been dark, Edmonds said: he had been walking around for hours, trying to make up his mind to go through with it, have the confrontation he wanted and yet dreaded with Karen. It was almost two in the morning before he'd finally raised enough determination to use the keys. He'd gone in.

When he entered the flat it was in a state of chaos. Clothing, personal effects, spilled over the floor. There was a little light coming from the kitchen. He walked towards the bedroom and at first he couldn't make it out: the blood was dark, the room sickly with the smell of death; the bundle on the bed was hardly recognizable as Karen O'Neill. He was in a state of shock. He had gone to the bed, tried to move her, to see if it was really her, if she was still alive . . .

'Two things,' Eric asked heavily, in the silence that followed. 'You say you moved her body. Do you recall touching anything in particular, apart from . . .'

Edmonds thought for a few minutes, head down, concentrating on a scene he had tried to wipe from his mind ever since he had left the flat. He nodded, and Eric's heart dropped. 'There was something on the bed, beside her. An object . . . heavy, dark wood. A carving of a Maori warrior . . . its eyes sort of gleamed. I picked it up, moved it as I reached for her . . .'

The 'blunt instrument' Lyle had mentioned. They'd have Edmonds's print on it. Bad.

'Secondly, the keys. What did you do with them?'

'I kept them.'

'You *what*?'

'I didn't think,' Edmonds protested uncertainly. 'I was distressed, shaken . . . scared. I'd put the keys in my pocket when I entered the flat; I closed the door behind me when I left and I just . . . forgot about the keys.'

'And later?'

'I . . . I just didn't use those clothes. They . . . reminded me—'

Eric stared at him. The man had been incredibly stupid, and naïve, and careless: a combination that suggested innocence. But the police had motive, opportunity, and evidence in the form of the print on the Maori warrior. 'Who has the keys now?' Eric asked.

'The police,' Edmonds said unhappily. 'They took my clothes.'

Eric sighed and shook his head. 'One last thing. When you entered—or left—the apartment, did anyone see you?'

There was a short silence; Edmonds's mouth was set grimly. He no longer wanted to talk about this matter: he could see the case building up against him more clearly than he had previously envisaged. Reluctantly, he nodded. 'As I went in . . . there was a woman. She came into the hallway. I think she saw me.'

'What was she doing there?' Eric demanded.

'I think she was going into the other flat.' Edmonds looked at Eric, frowning. His heavy jaw was loose, anxiety pouching his eyes. 'It . . . it looks bad, doesn't it?'

Bloody bad, thought Eric.

3

The Salamander chill had begun to take effect. Share prices had begun to move, Eric noted in the financial press, and although it had occasioned little comment, the movement being put down to normal processes of the market, there was a hint in the *Financial Times* that a certain nervousness was becoming apparent in Gower and Rue.

Eric had no way of knowing whether the movement was due to Johnson's buying shares, or whether the 'fan club' had begun to pick up momentum, but Leonard Channing was wary in his conversation with Eric over the phone: he asked for a report on Johnson, but insisted on vagueness regarding the outcome.

The fact that Jim Edmonds was now held in police custody meant that Anne turned to Eric more for advice on the Graham acquisition during the following week. They had now produced their internal management accounts and Anne had taken financial advice on them from Morcomb Estates accountants: she also wanted Eric's views. He did what he could to help, but as far as he could see Edmonds's advice, even if given under stress at the time, had been sound. Together, he and Anne agreed that further pressure was necessary to agree the management involvement terms, and those other terms that might affect the valuation. Only then would they be able to negotiate sensibly on the actual purchase price to be offered for a major stake in Roger Graham, Ltd.

The Metropolitan Police had proved to be uncommunicative—and perhaps rightly so, when Eric attempted to obtain more information concerning the charges against Jim Edmonds. He was told coolly but politely that all would be revealed upon arraignment, and evidence presented in outline at the magistrates hearing.

162

It was likely that information could be obtained in Northumberland, but with Lyle having blocked him once, Eric was reluctant to try again: it could cause his old colleagues and contacts in the force trouble if he were to persist.

But there were other ways to make the approach. He rang Jackie Parton.

The little ex-jockey was a product of Scotswood, where he had learned in a tough school. He still maintained contacts in the West End because in his riding days he had become the image of local boy made good, and his cheerful, extrovert personality and refusal to turn away from his roots had retained for him a great deal of credibility. The end of his racing career had come with a pulped face and broken ribs, the legacy of a refusal to go along with track bookies who had attempted to fix a race, but that hammering he had taken on Dog Leap Stairs years ago had if anything enhanced his legend and his popularity.

For Eric he was a source of information—most of it by way of back stairs, all of it difficult to prise out through formal channels.

A pint of Newcastle Brown in the Hydraulic Engine was sufficient to re-open the acquaintance. Jackie Parton twinkled at him over the top of the beer glass. 'Well, bonny lad, it's been a while.'

'It has that, Jackie.'

'Big financier, these days.'

'Not exactly. Splitting my time, you could say.'

'And now there's this Edmonds character.' Parton scratched his narrow jaw thoughtfully. 'That Karen O'Neill woman, quite a looker, I'm told.'

'That's what I wanted to talk to you about, Jackie.'

'Thought it mebbe. So what do you want, Mr Ward?'

The pub was noisy; in the small room leading off the main lounge a billiards table had recently been installed and now shouts of laughter echoed through as one of the players fell far short of the skills shown by their televised heroes. Eric leaned forward across the table.

'I want to find out just what the prosecution case against Edmonds is. My own avenues into Morpeth are closed. The facts are these: they know he went to the flat, and they have the keys he used; I think they have a print of his; I want to know what else. Notably, will they be calling an inquiry agent he used as a witness? And will they be calling a witness who may have seen him enter the flat?'

Jackie Parton's eyes had clouded vaguely. He looked down at tough, lean, wiry hands, powerful hands that had ruled powerful mounts. 'Does the second witness exist?'

'I think so,' Eric said calmly. 'A woman. Same mews.'

Parton sniffed, his eyes still uncommitted. 'Sounds like they got Edmonds well booked. Did he do it, Mr Ward?'

Eric had expected the question. He met the ex-jockey's gaze frankly, knowing the man's local ethics, knowing Parton had to live in Newcastle, and retain his position of respect among his contemporaries. 'No, Jackie, I don't think he did.'

There was a short silence. Another roar of laughter came from the billiards room and from outside the Hydraulic Engine a tug siren sounded, echoing up from the flats on the bend of the river below the power station. Jackie Parton took a long pull at his beer. 'Aye, all right, I'll see what I can dig out. I'm owed a favour.'

'One more thing.'

'Aye, bonny lad, I thought there'd be more.'

'Karen O'Neill,' Eric said. 'She was a local lass. It was up here Edmonds met her. She's not been down in London long. I want to know about her—where she was brought up, her antecedents, the people she knocked around with. I want to get a picture of her, Jackie: I want to get to *know* her, if you understand me.'

The ex-jockey nodded, and finished his

165

pint. 'I know what you want, Mr Ward. You want to get inside her head.'

★   ★   ★

Eric visited Jim Edmonds again a few days later. The man seemed more cheerful, oddly enough, as though his conversation with Eric had removed some of the pressures from him. Possibly it was due to the fact that Eric seemed to believe his story, weak though it sounded.

Eric brought him up to date, told him he'd set certain inquiries in train, and went over Edmonds's account again, concentrating this time upon Karen O'Neill. He gained from Edmonds the now rather more detached view that maybe Karen O'Neill had been attracted to him, but not just for his physical presence: she had seen in him a money ticket, a route to a better, more luxurious life. Until she had gone to London.

At the conclusion of the interview Edmonds relaxed, leaned back in his chair and changed the subject. 'How are things going in the Graham acquisition?'

'As well as can be expected,' Eric replied cautiously, feeling like a doctor calming a patient. 'But I'm not sure you should worry about it: you've got more important things to think about.'

Edmonds grimaced. 'That assumes I *want*

to think about them. Fact is, I'm being treated pretty well here, Mr Ward, and I have time on my hands. I get the financial papers and I've time to read. I see, for instance, that the City is still in turmoil. Interesting movements in Salamander shares . . . no great panic yet, but . . . you want to go canny there, Mr Ward.'

'You think so?'

'The DTI are a bit sharp these days. Too many breaches of the City Code. I see they're sniffing at some new insider dealing rumours over the Reeves Grenham issue. There's a hint that some of the arbitrageurs were involved. But chasing after those shadows doesn't mean they won't also be watching Salamander. If there's anything odd going on there—like a sudden upward spiral on share prices, they could well get interested in the defence, even though they've already cleared the Gower-Rue bid in the first instance.'

Eric kept his features impassive. 'Thanks for the advice.'

Edmond nodded. 'I've also had time to think about the Graham acquisition. The distance this . . . situation . . . lends me makes me think more objectively, maybe. But if I were still advising Mrs Ward, I'd strongly suggest she presses Graham's on a performance-related purchase.'

'How?'

'I think when she comes to valuation and

decides a purchase price she should put forward an initial sum only, maybe linked to their immediate research and development needs.'

'Chris Graham won't enjoy that.'

'It's one reason to push it. I've had the feeling maybe he's been fishing for other offers in the City . . . Anyway, the additional payments thereafter could maybe be dependent upon pre-tax profit performance. You could make further payments calculated on a defined formula.'

'Over what period?' Eric asked.

'Maybe three . . . five years,' Edmonds suggested. 'After all, the assets you're getting in the Graham acquisition are only worth a relatively small part of the purchase consideration.' He paused. 'Will you pass the advice on, to Mrs Ward?'

'I'll do that,' Eric promised.

*   *   *

When he told Anne she pulled a doubtful face. In her opinion it would be a tough negotiating point: they would be unlikely to agree. Eric felt it was worth a try and spent several hours over the weekend, working on some models with her. They finally agreed upon a tactical approach: a meeting had been scheduled with the Grahams later the following week. 'It's nice to know that Mr

168

Edmonds is still bearing us in mind,' Anne said. 'He must have plenty to worry about. Is it still looking bad, Eric?'

'I would think it couldn't look worse.'

4

Eric was rather later than usual leaving Sedleigh Hall on the Monday morning. Consequently, he arrived in a hurry at the office and had to leave the Quayside almost immediately for a hearing in the county court. He walked up through Grey Street, past the station and Stephenson's statue, and got to the Registrar's office with a few minutes to spare. The solicitor acting for the other side was seated there, reading a newspaper. He looked up as Eric entered. 'Fun and games in the City, I see!' he exclaimed.

'I've not had time to see the news,' Eric replied. 'What—'

The usher appeared in the doorway. 'Are you ready, gentlemen?'

The hearing dragged on for most of the morning. At its conclusion Eric was engaged in a conversation regarding fees by a barrister's clerk and it was past lunch-time before he got back to his office. As he entered, the girl at the reception desk waved her hand. 'Oh, Mr Ward, there's a gentleman to see you. I said you'd be busy but he said he'd wait anyway. A Mr Parton.'

'I'll see him,' Eric said. 'Get some coffee

brewing, and slip out for some sandwiches, will you? Send Mr Parton straight up.'

Eric dumped his files on the desk and sat down; he felt weary, and there was a slight prickling at the back of his eyelids. The early morning drive, the hours in the courtroom; the problems of keeping several balls in the air at once . . . he'd need to go carefully, make sure the pressures were kept at bay.

There was a tap on the door, Jackie Parton entered and Eric waved him to a seat. 'I've got some sandwiches on the way. And coffee.'

Parton pulled a face, and Eric smiled. 'I've got whisky, if you prefer.'

The look on Parton's face convinced him and Eric rose, walked to the drinks cabinet and poured the ex-jockey a generous glass.

'Cheers!' Parton said.

'Good health. News?'

Parton smacked his lips appreciatively at the whisky. 'You could say, bonny lad, you could say. Where do you want me to start?'

'The interesting bits?'

'All interesting,' Parton suggested. 'First of all, me contacts tell me yes, they got a print on something that was used to hammer the O'Neill woman, and it's from Edmonds; second, they do have a guy called Stoker, private detective from Hammersmith, who'll testify for the prosecution that he found where O'Neill lived at Edmonds's request. Tie that in with the keys, and the guy's in

170

trouble: they can link him to the flat. They also got someone to talk about some noises that occurred on the stairs of Edmonds's flat a few weeks back: a quarrel between the pair of them in Newcastle.'

'They're really stitching it up,' Eric murmured.

'You're right there, hinny,' Parton agreed. 'But one thing they haven't got.'

'What's that?'

'The witness you mentioned . . . the one Edmonds thinks saw him enter the flat. She's not on the prosecution list.'

'Nothing to offer?'

'Or not prepared to say anything,' Parton suggested.

'Interesting . . .'

'I thought you'd think so, Mr Ward. I got her name, too. She lives just along the hall from O'Neill's flat.' He paused as the door opened and the sandwiches were brought in. He eyed them, sniffing slightly in appreciation. 'Prefer stotty cakes, mesel', but . . .'

'What's her name?' Eric asked, preparing to make a note.

'Calls herself Freda Sanderson. Don't know much more about her except she don't like coppers, maybe. However, Karen O'Neill, now, I got to find out more than a little about her.'

'Tell me,' Eric said.

171

It was a story disclosing not a unique experience: over the years Eric had come across many such young women, passing through lawyers' offices for one reason or another, or appearing in the courts. O'Neill had not been her real name: she had been born Karen Bellamy, in a one-parent family, the father having disappeared early in the parental relationship.

She had been raised near Wallsend, her mother having formed an association with a man working in the shipbuilding industry; when that relationship collapsed there had been a series of 'uncles', until at thirteen Karen herself had got involved, Jackie Parton explained with a wrinkling nose, with one of the 'uncles' in an unsavoury episode that only just managed to steer clear of criminal charges. Taken into care, Karen was later fostered with a family in Kenton, but she had left school at the first opportunity and drifted into several poorly paid jobs before undertaking some photographic modelling for a small-time photographer in South Shields. It was here she had got the idea of making a career for herself out of modelling but it had remained a dream until Jim Edmonds came along.

'She was young, beautiful and tough as old boots,' Jackie Parton said. 'The story is, she liked Edmonds, probably did think of marriage—but what she really wanted was excitement, money and a good time. My guess is she got fed up fairly soon with him, but managed to raise enough cash from him to get down to the Smoke.'

'Edmonds hasn't admitted lending her money.'

Parton shrugged. 'So the rumour goes. But she was certainly taking the guy for a ride . . . using him until something better came along. Like a modelling job in London.'

Carefully, Eric said, 'I've been told there was nothing to the modelling story. It's suggested she was just a whore.'

Parton blinked. 'I wouldn't know. I've had a sketch of her life on Tyneside; London's something else again. However, there is one very interesting little titbit you'll want to hear.'

The phone rang. Eric picked it up. It was a call from London. Eric agreed to take it. Parton looked at him, raised his eyebrows, gestured to the door but Eric shook his head.

'Ward? This is Leonard Channing. Are you alone?'

Eric glanced at Jackie Parton; the little man was reaching for a sandwich with his left hand, holding the half-empty glass of whisky in his right, fully occupied and concentrating.

'Yes.'

'We've got problems.' Channing's voice had a raspy, edgy quality to it.

'I've not heard.'

'Salamander. You'll have seen the shares started to rise.'

'Yes.'

'There's been a bad slide today, and it puts our whole strategy in trouble.'

'Why has it happened?' Eric asked.

There was a short pause; Eric could hear Channing's breathing, ragged, uncertain. 'Why? Some idiot at the DTI has nothing to do at the moment and has decided to take a closer look at the Salamander defence. At least, that's what we *think*. There's been no official announcement, but the rumour in the City is that the DTI *will* investigate.'

'We have no reason for concern, have we?'

'It's not a question of whether we've acted legally or not,' Channing snapped. 'I'm happy enough on that score. It's the fact that the Salamander defence will fall apart if the rumour isn't scotched; the shares will drop and the price won't freeze out the Gower and Rue bid.'

There was something unconvincing in Channing's tone; Eric hesitated, watching Jackie Parton munching at his sandwich unconcernedly. He had the feeling that Channing somehow was not disclosing the whole story. 'You're calling a meeting then, I imagine.'

'Everett is. Urgently. The war cabinet has to meet tomorrow to discuss these developments and develop a contingency plan to deal with the situation if the DTI rumour continues to have credence in the market place.'

'Tomorrow's difficult—'

'*Tomorrow*, Ward.'

Eric was silent for a moment. 'I'll see what I can do.'

'Two o'clock,' Channing snapped and put down the phone.

Eric looked at Jackie Parton.

'Trouble?' the ex-jockey asked.

'Isn't there always . . . ?' The prickling had returned, scratching at the back of Eric's eyelids. He reached for a sandwich and chewed it moodily, hardly aware of its taste.

'No way I can help, I suppose?'

'None. Thanks, anyway, Jackie. Look, unless there's anything else, I think we'd better leave it at this point. It's been useful—'

'I don't think we'd better leave it like that, Mr Ward,' the ex-jockey interrupted. 'There was one more juicy bit I was coming to—saving it for last, like.'

'In relation to Karen O'Neill?'

'That's right. You ought to know about it, before I leave you to get on with all this other business.' Jacky Parton finished his whisky in a gulp and set down his glass. 'Like I told you, I asked questions about her background. She was fostered out at Kenton, I told you. There was a family livin' out there at that time, moved later when they stopped putting

175

all their money into the business, like they did in the early years. Karen, she got friendly with one of the family . . . real close, like. Just before she left school it started, and for a few months afterwards, when she was drifting.'

'Go on.'

'I hear you and Mrs Ward, you're tied up with a company called Roger Graham, Ltd, in some way or another.'

'So?'

'It was that family that Karen Bellamy—as she was then—got friendly with. Or to be more precise, with the sons.'

'Tell me.'

'From what I hear,' Jackie Parton said, standing up to leave, and reaching for a sandwich to speed his way, 'there was a time Karen Bellamy and Chris Graham had a thing going which got very close. In fact, very, *very* close!'

CHAPTER FOUR

1

Eric had the opportunity to catch up on his reading of the financial press on his way down to London, and he could appreciate the nervousness that now must be appearing in the war cabinet. At least one commentator was speculating openly whether there had been illegal dealing in the movement of Salamander shares; two others suggested there might be some link between the DTI investigation into insider dealing in the Reeves Grenham issue and the interest being shown in the battle for Salamander.

It was a matter that was discussed immediately the meeting of the war cabinet opened at two o'clock. The pressure was getting to Paul Everett: however successful he might have been in the States and more recently in the UK, the situation in which he now found himself, with his stake in Salamander threatened, was making him edgy, and he was more than prepared to fasten blame.

'It seems to me one of our basic problems is the presence of an arbitrageur in our dealings here,' he snapped as the meeting began. He glared at Leonard Channing, as though willing him to dispute the matter. When Channing said nothing he turned his ire towards Hugh Nelson. 'Your name is being openly linked in the City with the Reeves Grenham DTI investigation into possible insider dealing.'

Hugh Nelson smiled thinly. 'It's never been a secret that I was and have been for months, in receipt of information—which I *paid* for—which could have placed me in a situation where I could have bought and sold early, before the market woke up to Reeves Grenham problems. It's another matter to suggest I used that information to gain—'

'There are plenty who are suggesting it!'

'Not to my face,' Nelson said coldly, a challenge in his eyes as he stared at Everett. 'And certainly not in print.'

'Your name is linked with it all,' Everett insisted stubbornly. 'And I've got a right to demand—'

'You've a right to *demand* nothing,' Nelson interrupted, a dangerous note in his voice. 'I'm here to help in the Salamander defence. My private interests—my arbitraging activities—are none of your business, and not in issue here.'

'They are if they're leading the DTI in our direction!' Everett snapped back. 'It's clear they're after you, want to get their hooks into you. What I want, and I think we have a right to it, is the knowledge that you're clean—'

'*Clean?*' Nelson sneered openly. 'What the hell is that supposed to mean? Who in this room can claim to be clean?'

The prickle was at the back of Eric's neck again. Leonard Channing leaned forward abruptly, his lean, ascetic features cool and unemotional. 'One moment. Let's not get too heated about this. I think what Paul is after is quite simple. He's concerned—*we're* concerned—that any interest the DTI have in the Reeves Grenham business doesn't spin off into an attack upon Salamander. That could happen, if the DTI feel that they can obtain evidence against *you* on an insider dealing issue—they could then step up into an investigation of the part you play in this war cabinet. That could lead to problems . . .' He was avoiding Eric's eye.

'So just what do you want from me?' Nelson asked coldly.

'An assurance, I suppose,' Channing replied in an even tone. 'This insider dealing—'

'There's no evidence to connect me with it,' Nelson said.

'There's no record of phone calls, or share-dealings which can be dated—'

'There's no evidence to connect me with the insider deals,' Nelson repeated. His tone had flattened, become more formal.

'Give a dog a bad name, and it sticks,' Paul Everett interrupted. He watched Nelson carefully for a few moments. 'In my experience there are always . . . loopholes, through which an inspector can squeeze. If you try to tell me that you've had no sticky finger dealings in Reeves Grenham I'd be inclined to say you're a liar, Nelson: that scene was too good for you to miss. But I'm not going to ask you that question. I'm going to ask you this: have you closed all the loopholes? And are you *certain* they're closed?'

Nelson hesitated. He had paled, and dangerous glints lurked in his eyes. 'I don't have to listen to this.'

'You do if you want to stay in this war cabinet.'

'I don't need . . .'

'You *do* need to stay,' Channing insisted quietly. 'If you leave now the whisper will very quickly go out that Salamander is nervous about your connection, and that'll give the DTI bloodhounds all the encouragement they need to *really* tear you apart!'

Nelson was cornered, and Eric could see he didn't like it. His lips were tight and his dislike of Everett and Channing clear. But he had got into this financial bed and it would serve him badly if he now had to leave it. He moistened his lips. 'There'll be a day . . .'

'Every dog has one,' Everett rasped. 'Talk to me now about loopholes.'

'Loopholes . . .' Hugh Nelson shook his head slowly. 'Salamander will have no trouble from me over Reeves Grenham insider dealings. There are no . . . All avenues have been closed.'

'Dead?' Everett insisted.

'Completely,' Nelson confirmed.

There was a long silence as Paul Everett stared at Nelson, holding his glance. Neither man was backing down, and though there was

180

a light sheen of sweat on Nelson's face his glance was steady and his hands still. At last Everett grunted, satisfied. 'All right. So let's get down to the real business. Channing?'

'Garden City Enterprises reacted favourably to Ward's visit, and bought in a considerable slice of Salamander shares. That purchase, together with others from within the fan club we established, pushed the share prices above the Gower-Rue bid and the market reaction was most favourable. However—'

'They're getting cold feet,' Nelson offered. 'It's obvious.'

Channing nodded. 'The market has slipped back again. The DTI rumours have shaken City confidence in Salamander and our fan club members who have made large commitments have been ringing in—'

'Chicken-livered bastards!' Everett snarled.

'They're concerned that if the price slides much more they'll be left in a bad position; moreover, if Gower and Rue push any more and Salamander collapses, their re-purchase guarantees will be worth next to nothing.'

'What do they think this is, a kindergarten?' Everett demanded. He released a stream of obscenities, and then glared at Nelson. 'Okay. So you're part of the problem. How do we handle things now?'

'We increase the chill,' Hugh Nelson replied. His tone was confident, edged with scorn. 'This is a flurry: you know how the City panics. It's the time to buy in fact. There's only one way you're going to close down the possibility of a DTI investigation, and that's by closing down the deal as quickly as possible. Once the Salamander defence works and Gower and Rue walk away again the DTI will back off—it'll be none of their concern, the shareholdings will have been finalized, a commercial deal will have been concluded.'

'Closing down the deal . . . easier said than done,' Channing offered. 'You say we should increase the chill, but the financial package I've presented already stretches to your issue limits: junk bonds—'

'We need a new financial investment,' Nelson said crisply, 'and we need to make some additional offers.'

'Investment?' Channing queried. 'From where?'

Nelson glanced at Everett and smiled coldly. The managing director of Salamander stared back and some kind of silent message passed between them. After a few moments Everett looked at Channing. 'From a merchant bank?' he suggested quietly.

There was a long silence. Eric waited, feeling the pressure being put on Channing and waiting to see how the man would react. He had no choice, really, but he would have to consider it.

Channing hesitated. 'It's a . . . possibility,' he admitted.

Eric could hardly believe his ears. 'Channing—'

'It *could* be a possibility,' Channing continued thoughtfully, 'if the terms were right.' He ignored Eric as he went on, 'The share price would have to be negotiable, of course, and the re-purchase guarantees suitably framed.'

'Details,' Everett murmured wolfishly. 'Let's talk about principles.'

'In principle—'

'Channing, wait a minute,' Eric insisted, breaking in before decisions and commitments were made. 'You have no authority to make such a commitment.'

Channing's head did not turn. 'As senior partner in Martin and Channing—'

'You'd need the board's support before you could commit Martin and Channing funds to this project!'

'There's no time for that,' Everett snapped angrily. 'This is a *today* decision—we've got to close down any possibility of DTI involvement!'

'I think that if we entered a *suitable* agreement,' Channing said, 'I would be able to swing the board behind me later. Even so, the amount of funds available would hardly bring about the desired effect. Nelson, you talked of other steps—'

'I think we'll have to consider an off-shore operation, maybe through Guernsey where purchasing—'

Eric rose to his feet. 'Wait a moment, Nelson. I can't countenance this.'

'You can't *what?*' Everett demanded, leaning back in his chair.

Eric was cool, unmoved by Everett's bluster. 'I'd better make my position clear. I understand I was asked to attend this war cabinet as an adviser and as a representative of Martin and Channing. So I'm advising . . . *now*. You've already sailed close to the wind with the deals you've struck with the fan club. In my view you're in breach of City practice: such deals should be disclosed. That's your problem. The re-purchasing agreements . . . well, I've not been given any details so I can't comment, but I think they could well be not just a breach of the City Code—they could well be illegal in themselves. I've kept a low profile so far because I see my position largely as that of an observer, but now that the situation of Martin and Channing has been brought into it I have to make a stand. Channing is a senior member of the board, but he can't speak for the board—'

'Any more than *you* can!' Channing flashed.

'And consequently any commitment he might make in the name of Martin and Channing is one I can't go along with.'

There was a short silence. 'It seems,' Everett said icily, 'there's a couple of things here you can't go along with, Ward. Lost the stomach for a fight?'

'I'm a lawyer. I'm in practice. I can't support illegal practices.'

'Show me one,' Nelson murmured.

'They're bordering—'

'The best answer for us all would be if you were to withdraw,' Everett cut across him. 'That way, everyone's *conscience* would be at ease.'

The sneer was not lost on Eric. He looked at his senior partner. 'Channing?'

Leonard Channing had lost some of his customary urbanity. He seemed to be struggling with his feelings: there was a glint of cupidity in his eyes at the thought of his bank taking advantage of the position Salamander found itself in, but there was nervousness too: Ward had been placed in the war cabinet as a compliance officer and his advice right now was that the war cabinet was hardly complying with the City Code, or possibly, legal rules. The question in Channing's mind was—if Eric left the war cabinet, could Channing swing the Martin and Channing board behind him at the relevant time? Eric watched while the man struggled with the problem. At last, after a long silence, Channing raised his head and looked Eric straight in the eyes. There was a

185

confidence about his tone, even if it was not supported by the lurking doubts at the back of his eyes.

'I don't think we need detain you here any longer, Ward,' Channing said.

Eric nodded briefly. He picked up his papers and left.

★   ★   ★

Eric could not be certain he had taken the right course. He was in the war cabinet as a Martin and Channing appointee, and he had now left Channing with a free rein. The board *might* later see that as a dereliction of duty. The trouble was, he couldn't be certain whether illegalities were taking place because he hadn't had sufficient information about the fan club. And he himself had 'recruited' Garden City Enterprises to the flag of Salamander, albeit under instructions from the war cabinet.

He gnawed at the problem in his room at the club that evening, before he went around to see Jim Edmonds, on remand. His own understanding of the City Code was somewhat sketchy: he was no company lawyer. He was still mulling it over when he met Jim Edmonds in the interview room that evening.

Briefly he ran over what Jackie Parton had told him about Karen. Edmonds took the

186

information woodenly. He agreed he'd known little about Karen's background: it hadn't been important to him at the time. He knew nothing about her living in Kenton and when Eric told him about the old association with Chris Graham, Edmonds paled.

'I didn't know about that.'

'The evening at Perastino's—the way he was almost pestering her—didn't you discuss that?'

Edmonds shook his head. 'It bothered me . . . I told you. It . . . it was the reason for our quarrel. But she never told me she knew the family—'

'And they kept pretty quiet about it,' Eric said grimly. 'They closed ranks, of course, later. The old man never liked her, I guess, and . . .' He hesitated. 'Karen never admitted *knowing* Chris Graham previously?'

'No,' Edmonds confirmed. 'And like I told you . . . our argument turned to . . . making love.'

Eric frowned. He was thinking back to something said at Sedleigh Hall. Roger Graham had been angry at his youngest son's failure to turn up. Nick Graham had covered up something that day; he'd said Chris was in London on business. But the old man had used the word *infatuation*.

'Do you think,' Eric asked slowly, 'there's a possibility that the relationship between Chris and Karen never came to an end?'

Edmonds stared at him, his wispy moustache looking sad at the very suggestion. 'I can't . . . I can't believe that. When she came to the States . . .'

'She could have been keeping him dangling until she had you firmly hooked.'

Edmonds didn't like it. He shook his head. 'I can't believe that. Her attitude to me . . .'

Lovers could be blind, Eric thought. 'If not a continuing relationship, maybe it sparked to life again at Perastino's—for Chris Graham, at least. Maybe his visits to London weren't for business . . . but to pursue Karen.'

Edmonds remained silent. After a little while, Eric sighed. 'All right, now about this other woman, the one in the lobby of the building. *Did* she really see you?'

Edmonds wrinkled his brow, happier with ascertainable facts that did not touch too closely on raw emotions. 'I . . . I feel sure she did. She looked straight at me. I was anxious, you see; shaky. I just stood there looking at her, foolishly . . . I'm *certain* she saw me.'

'So why isn't she telling the police?'

'Have they asked her?'

'I can't imagine they'll not have asked her,' Eric replied.

'I'm sure she saw me. Why she hasn't come forward, I don't know . . .'

They went over Edmonds's story again and Eric explained the procedures that would now be followed over arraignment and proofs.

Then, finally, at the end of the interview Eric leaned back hesitantly and looked at Edmonds. 'You know I'm involved in the Salamander defence?'

'You have problems?'

There was a short silence, and Edmonds smiled wanly. 'Confidential, hey? Well, I'm in no position to disclose information. Want to talk to me about it?'

Eric did. The man was an acquisitions expert, well used to the techniques, demands and rules of the City in merger and acquisition situations. It could be useful, bouncing off him some of the anxieties Eric felt. Edmonds listened, nodding from time to time, smiling occasionally. When Eric had finished, Edmonds sighed.

'The chill, hey? The Salamander chill. Never heard it put quite that way before, but a good enough way to describe the defence operation.' He was silent for a little while. Then he said slowly, 'I think you were right to make your play, and pull out. They'll be nervy, now. And I'm pretty certain there'll be shenanigans behind the scenes you won't know about. The only way you'll find out, though, is through unofficial channels. There's a guy I know . . . a financial journalist. It's taking a chance, but he's discreet, and if you give him a few titbits, he could feed them to certain people and come up with a few answers.'

'What people?'

'Some of the Salamander fan club,' Edmonds said. 'They're in big trouble, if it all hits the fan.'

'A tricky strategy.'

'You could try it, even so. His name is Cooper. If he unnerves a few of the people in the fan club with information he *seems* to have, they could give him a lot more than he really has to start with. Try it?'

'I'll think about it.'

Eric was still mulling it over when he took dinner in his club that evening. It was a high risk strategy, and one that could blow up in his face. He glanced at his watch, uncertainly. Cooper . . . If he rang him, talked to him for a while, using Edmonds's name . . . It could bring down the whole Salamander defence, and that was a risk: on the other hand, it could give Eric the basic information he needed to confront Everett, Nelson and Channing, in the interests of Martin and Channing. A direct approach to the Martin and Channing board would be useless: they would want facts, and they'd back Leonard Channing in the absence of facts.

Deciding, Eric pushed back his chair and rose to his feet.

'*Ward!*'

Eric turned. A matter of feet away from his table stood Chris Graham, eyes wide in surprise, fair hair falling boyishly over his forehead. Eric stared at him, and a guilty flush stole across the young man's face, as though he had been caught out in some nefarious act. 'Ward,' he said, 'what are you doing here?'

'This is my club,' Eric said evenly. 'I didn't know you were a member.'

'Well . . . about six months ago . . .' Graham was ill at ease. He glanced around uncertainly. 'I . . . I've got a friend, expected here for dinner . . . Nice to see you. I'd better get to my table . . .'

He moved away. Eric walked towards the lobby. A coincidence, Graham being a member of this club. And he had been coming to London recently: Eric recalled Nick Graham saying so, that evening at Sedleigh Hall. London. On business. Seeking other bidders?

Leaving the club, Eric stopped to make a call to the financial journalist, Cooper, whom Edmonds had mentioned. The call began warily, but lasted for some twenty minutes. At its conclusion, Eric told the porter to charge the call to his room. Then, hesitating, he said, 'I believe Mr Chris Graham is staying at the club at the moment. How long is he booked in for?'

'One moment, Mr Ward . . . Three days, sir. He arrived this afternoon. Shall I call—'

'No, not necessary, I'll meet up with him later,' Eric replied evasively.

He walked out into the late evening air. It was cool along the Embankment and the Thames glittered under the lights, moving darkly and menacingly towards the distant coast. He had a great deal to think about: the wisdom of having contacted this man Cooper; what would happen to the Salamander chill if someone was indiscreet; the continued presence of Chris Graham in London and the purpose of his present and past visits; the impact a new bidder might have upon Anne's proposals for the acquisition of Roger Graham, Ltd.

And Jim Edmonds. The case against Jim Edmonds in the murder of Karen O'Neill. Eric quickened his step, turned away from the river and headed for the brighter lights away from the Embankment, where he would be able to hail a taxi.

There was a question niggling at him: this was as good a time to have it answered, maybe.

He climbed into the taxi he obtained and gave the driver the address.

'Hey,' the driver exclaimed in interest. 'Ain't that where that fashion model got choked?'

★　　★　　★

It was surprisingly easy getting into the building. The external door was locked and

Eric guessed that if he requested admittance it would be denied, so he waited, standing just across the road from the entrance. After some twenty minutes a man parked his car nearby and walked towards the door. He reached it, inserted a key and Eric walked swiftly across: as the man entered and was about to let the door swing shut Eric put out his hand and with a muttered 'Excuse me,' entered the lobby behind him.

The man hesitated, glanced awkwardly at Eric but, seeing the confident way he walked across the lobby, turned and made his way towards the stairs to the right. He was out of sight quickly and Eric looked around him. The address and number he'd received were in his hand: the flat door was facing him.

He rang the bell.

There was a short silence. Then the peephole in the door was lifted and he was viewed critically. The voice that spoke had slurred tones. 'Who the hell are you?'

'My name is Ward.'

'Coppers, again?'

Eric raised his head slightly, making no reply, but it was taken for assent and, grumbling, the woman opened the door, 'What the hell do you want?'

'Just a few questions—'

She muttered an obscenity, turned away and Eric followed. 'I already told you bastards all that I had to, but it's typical, isn't it, you can't leave things alone, you got to keep pestering away. But I got nothing to add, so what's the point?'

She swung around to face him. She was short, about thirty years of age, with hair that was dark at the roots but exploding into blonde elsewhere. She wore a white shirtwaist blouse and dark blue skirt and she had been crying, dark smudges around her eyes from the destroyed mascara. She was also well on the way to becoming drunk and there was a shadow in the dark brown eyes that made Eric feel she was scared.

But not of him.

'You're Freda Sanderson?' he asked, in his best police voice, following the impression he had created in her mind.

'Who else would I be—crazy enough to stay in this place after what happened across the way?' She reached to the mantelshelf above the fireplace for her glass: it was whisky, and the bottle on the table was half empty. 'But I told you all I had to say about Karen's death.'

'You knew her, then?'

'A bit. We didn't socialize, like. Passed the time of day, more like.'

'You saw her the day she died?'

Something happened briefly to Freda Sanderson's mouth. She shook her head. 'No,' she lied.

'You didn't see her come home? You didn't

see anyone visiting her?'

'I told you before, I saw nobody.'

'Who are you trying to protect?' Eric demanded roughly.

'*Me!*' she flashed in a sudden anger and raised her glass as though she was about to throw it at him. 'I don't want nothing to do with all this, I never did, and I'm not getting involved now.'

'*Never did?*' Eric stared at her closely. 'What's that supposed to mean?'

She was confused. She turned away, took a pull at the whisky. 'It doesn't mean a thing. Just a way of talking.'

But it had been more than that. Eric moved forward to face her: she raised her face sullenly, but the shadowed fear in her eyes was stronger now. 'You say you saw no one at the flat that evening. What about other evenings? Did she have many visitors?'

'How would I know?'

'You're her neighbour.'

'I wasn't her keeper. And what she got up to was her business.'

'Was she a whore?'

Her eyes widened and she stared at Eric as though she began to see him clearly for the first time through the haze of alcohol. 'You're not a copper! I said all I had to say to them. I don't know a thing about Karen O'Neill, or who killed her. Who the hell are you?'

Eric hesitated. 'I'm a solicitor. I'm

representing the man who's been charged with her murder.'

Freda Sanderson chewed her lip. The flaring fear in her eyes had diminished. She stared at Eric, undecided, and the indecision grew as though other conflicting facts and ideas crowded in upon her. She shook her head, as if trying to clear it, reach peace again. 'You'd better go.'

'I'm trying to get at the truth. I don't believe Jim Edmonds killed her. He was her fiancé—'

'You crazy? Fiancé? He must have been nuts!'

'Why?'

The woman struggled with her thoughts again, regretting the scornful outburst. 'A solicitor . . .'

'Why was Edmonds a fool?' Eric insisted. 'Because he trusted Karen O'Neill? Because she *was* a whore?'

'She wasn't! She was . . . all right.' Freda Sanderson finished her drink and glared moodily at the empty glass. 'They asked me that . . . they said she was on the game, like she couldn't have afforded that flat on the bits of work she picked up in London. Bloody coppers . . . I've no time for them.' She squinted suspiciously at Eric. 'How come I thought you was one at the door?'

'I used to be a policeman once, years ago.'

She gave a short, barking laugh. 'And the

196

mark never disappears, is that it? I'm damned
. . . but a solicitor, hey? Maybe that's what I
need, a bloody good lawyer . . . or a bloody
good drink.'

Eric watched her as she moved unsteadily
to the bottle on the table, and poured herself
a drink. 'What are you scared of, Freda?' he
asked quietly.

'Scared of?' She giggled suddenly. 'Other
people's business. And that's what lawyers
are good at, isn't it? Minding other people's
business?'

'And keeping them out of trouble,' Eric
replied in an even tone.

'I'm in no trouble.'

'You're scared of something. Is it to do
with Karen? Tell me, if she *wasn't* on the
game, and if there wasn't all that much
modelling work for her, how *did* she afford
the flat?'

'That was her business.'

'But she talked to you about it.'

'*No!*'

The answer came too quickly and too
vehemently. She knew it, and the fear was
back in her eyes. Something was worrying her
badly, and it wasn't the thought of
entanglement with the police. Eric considered
what she had already said in her
whisky-slurred carelessness. 'You never did
want to get involved with Karen . . . but you
knew her, you liked her . . . and you knew

what she was doing . . .'

'I didn't say that,' Freda Sanderson said sullenly.

'You're afraid whatever she was up to might rebound on you,' Eric suggested. 'Was it something to do with her death?'

There was a long silence. She kept her head down, her eyes averted, and she was shaking slightly, desperate to get control of herself. Eric tried one more tack. 'If you need a lawyer—'

'Like a hole in the head, I need a lawyer,' she said with sudden spirit. 'You better go.'

There was nothing more he could do. Eric nodded and turned. He began to walk to the door. A sudden thought struck him. He paused. 'Tell me, does the name Chris Graham mean anything to you?'

She stared at him, her mouth working loosely. One hand strayed to her throat in an involuntary gesture. 'I . . . I never went in for names,' she replied.

Eric opened the door. He stood there for a moment, looking at her, and he had the feeling she didn't want him to go: the dark shadows were back in her eyes, and she was afraid of being alone. He waited, and she watched him, confused and indecisive.

'Remember,' he urged her quietly. 'If you think I can help . . .'

For a moment he thought he had got through to her. The sullen features began to crumple and tears welled up in her eyes, glittering on her smudged eyelashes. But doubt came back again, and uncertainty. 'I . . . I'll think about it. You . . . you said your name was . . .'

'Ward,' Eric replied swiftly and, dragging out his wallet, extracted his card. 'You can get me at this office, and for the next few days I'll be staying at my club. This is the address . . .' He wrote it down quickly, on the back of the card. 'You can catch me there during the next couple of days.'

Some of the toughness was coming back to her mouth. 'I'll bear that in mind, Mr Ward. Make sure you close the outside door behind you.'

2

'The Salamander chill. That's what they're calling it, hey? I like it. And I'm sure as hell no one who's at the receiving end does!'

Phil Cooper was built like a tank. His suit seemed to strain at the seams and his muscular shoulders threatened mayhem to his jacket. His square-shaped frame was topped by a similarly constructed head: solid, chunky, square. His eyes were a bright ice-blue, but his smile had a warm, genuine look to it. He was known to be shrewd and reckoned to be discreet and Eric liked the look of him. He was too wary to be taken in by a superficial impression, however, and here in his club, in a corner of the library, he was still weighing up what the financial journalist could be trusted with.

'So what have you got for me?' he asked.

Cooper screwed up his eyes thoughtfully. 'Beyond the impact of the strategy you've outlined for me—the chill—not a great deal. I'd need a great deal more information before I could help very much.'

'Such as?'

'Names,' Cooper announced blandly. 'I'd need to talk to people.'

'If you talked to them, their cover would be blown and the strategy could collapse.'

'It's a risk for Salamander, certainly,' Cooper agreed. 'But you've already taken a risk talking to me at all. I'm still not certain why you've done so.'

Eric hesitated. He'd gone this far; it was pointless holding back now. 'It's . . . it's because I'm concerned that maybe . . . irregularities have occurred.'

'Spoken like a lawyer.' Cooper nodded thoughtfully, his eyes keen on Eric. 'I guessed that was so . . . not least from the reaction to the few phone calls I've already made.'

'You've not disclosed—'

'No sources, no comebacks.' Cooper held up a placatory hand. 'But look, before we go further, I got to tell you we have a deal to reach. I agreed over the phone to play cool and set no real hares running scared. That's fine. But if we now go further—and I don't think we can just *stop*—there's a price on my discretion and silence.'

'Isn't there always?' Eric asked sardonically.

Cooper hardly blinked. 'The price is, I want an exclusive on all the information when—or if—it blows.'

It was a good bargain. Eric nodded. 'Provided *I* decide when—or if—the whistle goes,' he insisted.

'It's a deal.'

'So, what have you got?' Eric asked again.

Cooper sighed, leaned back into the comfort of the leather armchair, which echoed his sigh, and took out a pocket notebook. 'The City is a vulnerable place,' he said, 'without really knowing it. The assumption is that all is very secret, close to the chest, but that's not the way it can *ever* be. There are always avenues . . . Take the Reeves Grenham thing, for instance. There's a few guys going to catch a cold over that. The DTI are ferreting around and one of these days they'll get their hands on some paper, some notes, some *details*, simple enough in themselves, maybe, which will open up the whole can of worms. And this Salamander thing is the same.'

'How do you mean?'

'It's all about money, and power,' Cooper

201

explained. 'And that means people. And people are human. They're greedy. They get scared. And in the right circumstances, when the pressure comes on they'll run for cover. When they do that they do foolish things: they expose themselves, their backs, their papers, and the doubtful deals come out into the open.'

'And Salamander is like that?'

'The chill, as you call it, is a sound strategy, and it's got Gower and Rue worried. That's clear. But the whole thing is skating on thin ice. And it depends upon one assumption.'

Something cold moved in Eric's stomach. Right from the beginning of the war cabinet discussions he had felt there was something wrong, something that didn't quite fit, something missing in the equation Nelson and Everett had presented.

'What's the assumption?'

'The marketplace.'

'I don't understand.'

'There's got to be an assumption that the market will continue to move upwards. If it doesn't, the whole of the strategy collapses.'

'That simply means Salamander will lose in its defence, and Gower and Rue will win in their takeover bid.'

Cooper shook his head slowly, his ice-blue eyes hard. 'No. I think it means more than that. It means the roof falls in on everyone concerned.'

Eric leaned back and watched the financial journalist sprawled awkwardly in the leather armchair. 'You're not spelling out the problem.'

Cooper tried a shrug, and the armchair groaned. 'Maybe, but it's because I haven't got all the facts. You have. But on the few names you've given me so far, and my review of the market movements, together with your description of the chill . . . okay, let me ask you straight. Does it include re-purchase agreements, your fan club dealings?'

Eric hesitated, uncertain. That uncertainty was confirmation enough.

Cooper nodded. 'Okay, you don't need to tell me. I assume it does. So, this is the scenario, as I see it, and this is the danger the whole strategy can face. You're in rough waters, my friend, and the rocks are sharp.'

'Tell me.'

'Salamander has established a fan club. It's busy *persuading* the members to buy in shares and push the price up. I don't want to know what the persuasion is, but I can guess. And it won't just be re-purchasing agreements.'

'Go on,' Eric said levelly.

'The shares will lie in these safe houses, but that can only stay that way for a period: the fan club will want to get rid of the holdings in due course to take their profits once Gower and Rue ride off into the sunset. The key to that *must* be that Salamander will have to buy in their own shares. And *that* is illegal.'

'Not if the shareholders give their approval.'

'But they'll never be asked,' Cooper said blandly. 'The whole strategy surely depends upon their never being told.'

The coldness in Eric's stomach was spreading. 'Why are you so certain of that?'

'Because my guess is that Salamander is already overstretched on its junk bond issue. The financial package that's been raised by your own merchant bank—and the market tells me this—*must* be as far as Salamander can go. Therefore, how the hell is it going to be able to afford to re-purchase the shares in a month's time, or whenever? As soon as it goes to the shareholders for approval of the purchase there'll be all hell to pay. Questions will be asked, the strategy called into question, the ethics and legality of it all will be looked at by the DTI . . . No, my friend, the Salamander chill is based upon an entirely different end game.'

'Which is?'

'The assumption about the market. It *has* to move up. While it does, the legal trap will be avoided. In a rising market the "overhang" of stock can be made to disappear quietly, covered in the accounts by the profits that Salamander itself will show in its shareholdings. The evidence will just disappear and the DTI won't be able to do a thing. The buying-in will cover, and more than cover, the shares lying in the safe houses. It's a strategy Everett has used before. Offer a guarantee, and pay for it out of the profits you make before the guarantee gets called in. Classical. Provided the market stays on an upward spiral. But what's going to happen even then, when the dividend cheques go out?'

'I don't understand.'

Cooper smiled wolfishly. 'It's the *avenues* I told you about; the bits of paper; the seemingly inconsequential, unimportant things that suddenly get an inflated importance. Take a look at Salamander accounts. They're shortly due to issue dividend cheques on all their shares. Now, will any of the shareholders become embarrassed when they receive those cheques?'

'Why should they?' asked Eric, puzzled.

'Because, *maybe*, some of them have taken up more than five per cent of the shareholding. And not disclosed it. And that means *they're* in trouble, and the DTI will have evidence of a breach of the City Code, and everyone will start to run for cover and mistakes will be made and the market will drop . . .'

'I got an assurance that no purchases would be made in excess of five per cent,' Eric said.

'An assurance? From whom?' Cooper grinned. 'From Everett, when his back is against the wall? Can you really *rely* on that assurance?'

★   ★   ★

'Can we?'

There was a long silence. Eric waited with the phone in his hand while Leonard Channing collected his thoughts. Eric could hear the rasp of the merchant banker's breath, rattled, uncertain, defensive under Eric's demands.

'Now look here, Ward, I think you're over-reacting. I—'

'Can we rely on the assurance given?' Eric repeated.

'In all matters like this discretion is necessary. I haven't personally checked the individual holdings. The information hasn't been given to me and—'

'When I left the meeting,' Eric cut in coldly, 'you were in the process of agreeing a substantial investment in Salamander by Martin and Channing.'

There was a short silence.

'Did you go through with it?' Eric asked.

'Ward, when you walked out of that room—'

'Did you go through with it?'

'If you think that just because you're a

lawyer you can start browbeating me in this way, I've got news for you—'

'And I've got news for you, Channing!' Eric interrupted. 'I've reason to believe this whole defensive strategy could blow up in our faces. We've been given assurances that may or may not have been kept. It's always been a high risk strategy that bordered on illegality, and it now looks as though it has strayed over—and seriously, in its basic assumptions. Now that's something Martin and Channing can't afford to get involved with. And it's *certainly* something which they can't *invest* in!'

'Ward—'

'You've got a choice, Channing. Either you call an immediate meeting of the war cabinet, or I go over your head and make a report, at once, to the full board of Martin and Channing.'

'Ward, you can't push me into—'

'Channing, you've got your choice,' Eric said grimly. *'Make it!'*

3

The following morning Eric scanned the newspapers carefully. The market was uneasy, dithering. It was clear there was considerable uneasiness about rumours of DTI activity, but the initial impact was over, and Salamander shares had begun to climb again. There was a good prospect, Eric guessed, that the chill would work but he also knew that the small rise in the share prices could be part of the Salamander war cabinet gamble, made in his absence. And supported by a share purchase on behalf of Martin and Channing.

He turned quickly to the article written by Phil Cooper. He breathed a sigh of relief: the financial journalist had kept his word. It was a wide-ranging article that concerned itself with OPEC and oil prices: it made no mention of DTI activity and contained nothing that might affect Salamander, nor demonstrate the holding of insider information regarding the Salamander defence. The war cabinet would, therefore, be unaware of Eric's stand in detail, and the institutional investors would not get nervous and upset the boat.

At ten o'clock he was still waiting in his club for a phone call from Leonard Channing. It finally came, a few minutes after ten.

'Ward?'

'Yes.'

'It's agreed.' Leonard Channing's tone was crisp, and cold. 'We shall meet at two this afternoon. I may add . . . they don't like it.'

'The thought doesn't make me tremble.'

There was a short pause. 'I think you're making a mistake, Ward.'

'In my view, you've already made one. I'm assuming your commitment of Martin and Channing funds has helped the slight rise in

Salamander this morning.'

Channing ignored the remark. 'You're raising this wind at a bad time. There's every prospect that the chill is working. From information supplied to me by Everett it seems the institutional investors in the fan club are almost all committed, with two large purchases to be made before close this afternoon. Coming late like that they'll push the price up beautifully and on the morning call we could see Gower and Rue running scared. They'll be out to skin you this afternoon, my friend—'

'I can't imagine that'll cause you to lose any sleep.'

'You're a representative of Martin and Channing—'

'That's why I'm demanding this meeting.'

'It's still not too late to cancel it,' Channing suggested softly.

'Two o'clock,' Eric said. 'Let's make sure we're all there.'

Leonard Channing was breathing hard. He would be struggling with his temper: Eric visualized him, sitting bolt upright in the leather chair behind his ornate, polished desk. Channing cleared his throat. 'As you will. However, the point has been made to me quite forcefully by Everett that we have to move carefully. The market is in a delicately poised situation right now. Gower and Rue are getting nervous. The last thing the war

209

cabinet would want at this juncture is for it to appear that Salamander is losing its nerve. A hastily called meeting of the kind you're demanding could give us a bad press—'

'The meeting's *necessary*, Channing!'

'I'm not disputing that. It's the *location* that's concerning us! If we meet at Salamander, or at the offices of Martin and Channing, there's always the danger that some smart financial journalist will get to know about it and put two and two together to reach a conclusion damaging to the defence strategy. Consequently . . .'

'Yes?'

'It might be better if we had not a formal meeting as such but . . . well, a lunch date, say . . .'

It made sense. Eric could appreciate the point. 'All right,' he agreed. 'Where would you suggest as an *innocent* location?'

'Not only that, Ward, but *secure*. A restaurant would mean the denial of privacy. Your club, on the other hand, or mine . . .'

'My club,' Eric said crisply. 'I'll make the arrangements right now for a private room. Lunch, then, Channing, at two.'

'A little uncivilized,' Channing said coolly, recovering his customary urbanity at last, 'but we'll be there.'

'I look forward to seeing you all,' Eric replied. He did not add, *with pleasure*.

There was time now to prepare his brief. He
went over again in his mind, and in notes,
just what Phil Cooper had given him. He
sketched out the possible scenarios and
checked in the club library—where they held
a small but useful collection of law books,
many out of date, but generally of some
utility—on certain aspects of company law
and City practice.

Time passed swiftly; it was almost twelve
before he realized he hadn't even had a coffee
that morning. He walked down the wide
marble staircase to the smoking-room where
he knew coffee would still be being served.
He sat down, ordered coffee in the half empty
room.

It arrived at the same time as Chris
Graham.

The youngest of the directors of Roger
Graham, Ltd, stood in front of Eric and
stared down at him. He wore a dark grey
business suit, pale blue shirt, and a dogged
expression. His fair hair was carefully
brushed and there was a certain light in his
eyes that suggested to Eric the young man
was imbued with a feeling of triumph.

'Mr Ward?'

'Mr Graham.' Eric nodded formally.

'May I join you for a few minutes?'

'I . . . I have a meeting to prepare for,' Eric

211

said warily.

'So do I.' The glint was brighter in Chris Graham's eyes. 'That's why I think we should talk a while.'

Eric gestured to the chair opposite him, across the small table. 'Coffee?'

Graham shook his head. 'My lunch appointment is for twelve-thirty. After that I'll probably be heading north with something to say to my father and brother.'

Eric nodded thoughtfully. 'I imagine this will have something to do with the Morcomb Estates acquisition proposal.'

Chris Graham nodded and leaned back casually in his seat, as though to bely the excitement he felt. 'Of course.'

'So why do you wish to talk to me?'

Graham grinned unpleasantly. 'I'm not fooled by the arrangement you have with your wife, Ward. It's perfectly clear to me you pull the strings: she might have the old man fooled, and maybe Nick too, but you're always *there*, aren't you, playing the innocent? But in reality—'

'You've got it all wrong, my friend,' Eric said.

Chris Graham paused, then shrugged. 'No matter, then, if you want to keep playing the game. Situation remains the same . . . What I wanted to ask you was to be frank with me. After all, we don't want to waste your time, do we?'

Eric glanced at his watch, pointedly. 'We do not.'

'All right. The facts are these. Morcomb Estates are still negotiating with us on the acquisition deal. One of the points raised for discussion has been a performance-related purchase.'

'I understand that is the case.'

'It's not acceptable.'

'To the board?'

'To me.'

'You're not the board of Roger Graham, Ltd.'

'But I carry *some* weight . . . and they'll have to listen if I come up with a straight cash purchase offer.'

Eric stared at him thoughtfully. 'Ah, you *have* been a busy little businessman, haven't you? Is that your lunch appointment this afternoon? To close a deal?'

'To agree details, yes.' Chris Graham's mouth was hard-edged. 'I've never made any secret of my lack of interest in the development of the firm, Ward. My view is that as far as the Graham family is concerned the company has run its course, it's had its best days. What it now requires to grow and expand further is new management, new drive, the thrust that an entirely new set-up would bring. To retain the existing management would be suicidal: Nick is still fighting Dad, and the firm could implode once Dad's out of the way because Nick . . . well, I have no confidence in him.'

'Your opinion is not necessarily well founded. But aren't we really talking about money?'

Chris Graham raised his head at the challenge in Eric's tone. 'All right, yes, we are. I'm not interested in the bloody company. Never have been—except as an asset that could be sold. If Nick gets working control everything will be ploughed back into the company and where does that leave me? It's all right for him, the company's his damned *life*!'

'Whereas all you want is money in your hot little hand.'

'Don't patronize me, Ward!'

The sudden sharpness of Graham's tone caused Eric to eye the man warily. He had never thought of Chris Graham as being anything other than weak. Now, suddenly, there was a toughness in the man's mouth, a determination he had not noticed earlier. Perhaps it was time to reassess Chris Graham; as the thought crossed his mind, something darker touched his memory. He held it for a few moments, suppressing it.

'All right, I won't patronize you, Graham, I'll just put it to you that you had an agreement with Morcomb Estates. It was, quite simply, that you would not negotiate with other prospective purchasers until final

214

details had been thrashed out—'

'Hold on! *I* didn't agree. The others might have done and that's their stupid business! How the hell can you negotiate a suitable and sensible price for a business if you don't check an offer against what the marketplace is prepared to raise?'

'You don't do business by breaking agreements.'

'Ethics? You're stuffing ethics at me, *you*, a bloody lawyer? Look, like it or not, I've *opened* negotiations with another bidder. It's looking good, in purchase price terms. What I want to know is this: how committed are Morcomb Estates to a performance-related purchase? I tell you, it's not on. So if you're serious about the acquisition you'll have to drop that as a main plank and concentrate upon a cash offer.'

'The rest of the family—'

'To hell with them! Is Morcomb Estates stuck with the performance-related principle of valuation?'

Eric smiled gently. 'Well, that's something you'll have to raise with my wife, isn't it?'

Chris Graham glared at Eric, glinting devils glancing deep in his eyes. The dark memory that had touched Eric's mind returned, and he said quietly, 'However, I'm glad to know that it was business that brought you to London on so many occasions recently.'

'What's that supposed to mean?'

215

Eric shrugged. 'I wondered whether there might have been other reasons.'

There was a short silence. The glint of anger had gone now, to be replaced by wariness. Chris Graham's lips were thin, careful. 'I'm not sure I follow you. What other reasons?'

'To meet a woman, maybe? An old friend, from a few years back?' Eric smiled gently. 'I mean, you *did* know Karen O'Neill in Newcastle didn't you?'

'At Perastino's—'

'No. Before that. Both you and Nick knew her . . . and you were pretty close to her, I understand. Did you renew the acquaintance, down here in London, after you met again at Perastino's?'

The colour was retreating slowly from Chris Graham's face. His gaze slipped past Eric, looking out to a point over Eric's left shoulder as though he were seeking old memories or older dreams. There was a stillness about his body that suggested control, however; he hardly seemed to be breathing. 'Have you been talking about me to the police?' Graham asked, his voice edged with anger.

'I represent Jim Edmonds. I'm pursuing my own line of enquiry. I—'?

Eric stopped. A uniformed waiter was approaching the table.

'Mr Ward?'

216

'That's right.'

'There's a telephone call for you, sir. A Miss Freda Sanderson.'

Freda Sanderson? Eric stared at the waiter in surprise. 'Where can I take it?'

'If you'd just step across to the lobby, sir.'

Eric glanced briefly at Chris Graham, before he muttered an apology and rose, leaving the table. He followed the waiter and was shown to a phone at the end of the reception desk.

'Yes?'

'Mr Ward? This is Freda Sanderson.' She sounded fluttery, nervous, out of breath as though she had been running. He guessed it was caused by something near to panic.

'What can I do for you?'

'Not that. It's what I can do for you . . . I didn't come clean the other day.'

'That was my guess.'

'I didn't want involvement . . . never did. And coppers . . . I'll have no truck with coppers. But now . . .'

'What's happened?'

'Nothing . . . except I been thinking a lot, and I'm scared, Mr Ward. It's nothing to do with me, and I didn't want to get involved—'

'You knew Karen O'Neill better than you admitted, didn't you?'

'Yeh. And though we each minded our own business . . . well, she wasn't a whore like the police say she was . . . once they get an idea

217

in their heads they kind of stick to it, don't they?'

Through thick or thin, Eric thought grimly, and often in the face of the evidence.

'She wasn't like that . . . but there was this guy—'

'Someone who visited her?' Eric asked.

'And . . . and paid for the flat.'

'Who was he?'

'I told you . . . I don't go in for names when it's not my business.'

'Did you ever see him?'

'Couple of times. I don't think he saw me . . . but I can't be sure, maybe he did once . . . but I saw him visit—'

'Freda, listen, we have to talk. I have an important business meeting shortly—'

'I can't get away for an hour or so . . . there's this other thing, you see . . .'

'Thing?'

'A book.'

There was a short silence. Eric felt cold, a slow excitement growing in him. 'What are you talking about, Freda?'

'It's a little notebook. It's got numbers in it. A few dates. A few names. I can't make nothin' of it but it belonged to Karen. She gave it to me, for safe-keeping.'

'*Safe-keeping?*'

'She said it was her insurance policy.'

Eric took a deep breath. 'Freda, listen to me. I know you're scared, I know you feel

218

you've got into something that may be dangerous. The best thing to do is to go—*immediately*—to the police—'

'*No!* I'll have nothing to do with coppers! I hate 'em and I don't trust 'em! If it suited them, they'd file this away, throw the notebook away, and I'd only be in trouble. No—you said lawyers was to help people. I want you to help me.'

Eric hesitated, glanced at his watch. 'All right. Listen. I have a meeting here, at my club. You have the address. Make your way here this afternoon; ask for me; I'll meet you here, at the conclusion of my meeting.'

'All right, Mr Ward, I'll—'

'And *Freda!*'

'Yeh?'

'Bring the book.'

Eric replaced the phone as she rang off. He stood there, staring at it woodenly for a while. Words tumbled around inside his head, confused phrases, ideas, a miscellany of possibilities that didn't make sense. For some reason, something that Phil Cooper had said teased at him; a remark of Paul Everett's; an attitude of the arbitrageur Hugh Nelson. He shook his head, unable to clarify his thoughts.

He went back to the smoking-room.

Chris Graham was no longer there.

CHAPTER FIVE

1

The private dining-room in Eric's club had been laid out with the degree of elegance that was traditional there. The table was covered in a white damask cloth; the table linen itself was spotless white with a pink rose motif; the cutlery glittered, highly polished, and it was with a sense of affront that the waiter discovered that none of the men present were particularly interested in food. Channing ordered a light salad; Nelson agreed to sole; Everett grunted he merely wanted coffee, while Eric found he was too edgy to want anything substantial. He ordered an omelette.

With his nose in the air and his back speaking his displeasure, the waiter left with the orders. There was a carafe of water on the table; Leonard Channing poured himself a half glass full, sipped it and turned to Eric in the silence.

'This is your show, Ward. You *demanded* this meeting. You had better get it started.'

'And you'd better have something important to say,' Everett added in an unpleasant tone. 'Channing made it clear that you as good as threatened him. I take it you're unhappy with the Salamander strategy—why the hell didn't you come up with some counter-proposals at the beginning?'

'I was never invited into this war cabinet in that capacity,' Eric replied. 'In Channing's words, I came in as a compliance officer, looking after the interests of Martin and Channing.'

'And then you walked out!'

'Because I felt that I hadn't been given sufficient information, and because I could not go along with what I thought was counter to the bank's interests.'

'All right,' Everett grunted. 'So now you're back. *Why?*'

Eric paused. 'Because I think I've now been able to obtain the information that none of you saw fit to reveal to me.'

Hugh Nelson turned his head to stare at Eric. He had seemed preoccupied up to this point, even rather bored by the necessity to be present, as though his thoughts were elsewhere. Now he was interested and so was Channing; more to the point, Everett's colour was rising as anger twisted his mouth. 'You've *obtained* information? From where? What questions have you been asking? If you've blown our cover, revealed the strategy, it could hand Salamander over to Gower and Rue on a plate! Damn you, Ward—'

'Look at the newspapers, Everett,' Eric snapped back. 'The shares are still rising.

Would that have been the case if I'd been indiscreet?'

'Mr Ward has a point,' Nelson agreed quietly. 'I think I would like to hear what he has to say. You've obtained information, you say. Precisely what?'

Eric glanced at the arbitrageur. 'Let's just say I've been given instruction from a qualified source on the working of the marketplace, and the way the Salamander defence fits into those operations.'

Hugh Nelson leaned back, his glance sharper now. 'So what has your . . . instruction led you to conclude?'

There was a short silence as Eric held his glance for a few moments and then looked around at the others. 'My conclusion is that you've all been part of a conspiracy that is probably illegal, and certainly unethical.'

Everett gave a wolfish smile, cynical, edged with ill-temper. 'I've had harder things than that said about me for years. It seems to me, Ward, you've just no stomach for a good tough fight.'

'In addition,' Eric said, ignoring Everett's comment, 'Channing has placed the bank in a position where it, too, could be subject to a DTI investigation for the part it played in stitching together the financial strategy.'

Channing turned cold, unimpressed eyes upon Eric. 'You're bluffing.'

'No,' Hugh Nelson said slowly. 'I don't

think he is. I believe he should, in everyone's interests, explain why he takes these views.'

Eric nodded. 'All right. Under the Companies Act 1985 it is a criminal offence for a company to buy its own shares in order to artificially inflate the value of the company.'

'That's not news. And we haven't been buying—'

'Similarly, it is a criminal offence for a company to give financial assistance *to others*, to help them buy the shares.'

'We've been over this,' Channing said testily. 'The fan club hasn't been given such support. Persuasion, the calling in of favours—'

'And the offer of re-purchase at a given price.'

'So?'

'So if it isn't *exactly* illegal, it's near it. If a secret deal is struck—such as to make good any losses sustained—it must be disclosed; otherwise the City Code on takeovers is broken.'

'I never said—'

'And if company funds are used, thereafter, actually to make good the losses, that is a separate and even more serious breach of the law.'

Hugh Nelson leaned forward, his features in repose, but his eyes watchful. 'But who says company funds—Salamander funds—

will be so used?'

'*Haven't they already been so used?*'

Everett glanced involuntarily towards Leonard Channing. The merchant banker sat still, his hands flat on the table in front of him. He was glaring at Eric, but some of the colour had gone from around his mouth. 'You'd better explain yourself, Ward.'

Eric shook his head, smiling contemptuously. 'But you must already have guessed, Channing: dammit, you *know* the City! Guessed, but didn't want to know so didn't ask?'

'What are you driving at?' Channing demanded angrily.

Eric pointed a stabbing, accusing finger in Everett's direction. 'The fan club is of *his* making. The persuasions were his. It's my guess some of those would have been illegal in nature: contract promises; trademark and patent rights; cash payments to groups to buy in at the right price. I wasn't told about any of that—were *you*, Channing? I was told it was to be done by re-purchasing agreements . . . legal, but only just.'

'This is just talk—'

'I don't think so. I think I'm right. But more critically, maybe, is the fact that the Salamander chill always depended on a market movement that might or might not have happened. And that's where the rub lies, Channing. The market has slipped in the last week. The question is: did all the fan club hold firm?'

Channing opened his mouth to say something, then closed it again. His eyes did not meet Eric's for several seconds; the time ticked away with agonizing slowness. Then he looked up. 'I have no such information.'

There was a sneering sound from Paul Everett. 'Come on, you never even asked!' The major shareholder in Salamander turned back to Eric. 'Okay, so what if the line did break. So what?'

The door opened; three waiters came in, carrying the plates ordered. The room fell silent as they served; when they had gone the food remained untouched. No one seemed interested; instead, tension crackled in the atmosphere about them as they awaited Eric's reply.

'If the line has broken—and I believe it has,' Eric said, 'Salamander will have had to buy those shares at a loss. It will not have had shareholder approval for the secret transaction; it will be in breach of company law; and every director who is party to such a transaction can be held personally liable and is subject to a sentence of imprisonment.'

'I'm not a director,' Hugh Nelson said casually, 'but I'm getting a rather uncomfortable feeling. I think you've been digging, Ward, haven't you?'

'Enough to piece together the picture as it

is, and as it's likely to be,' Eric replied. 'It was always a high risk strategy: that was explained. What I wasn't told was that the risk was too high to be backed by legal methods only: it always depended upon bending the law. For instance, the moment Gower and Rue back off there's going to be a scramble to sell Salamander shares to reap the profit while the price is high. Salamander will *have* to buy its own shares then, even if it already hasn't done so. In doing so, Salamander will be certain to lose money—without disclosing this in the end of year accounts.'

'If the shares continue to rise,' Everett insisted, 'the rush won't occur.'

'And that's the big gamble,' Eric said. 'It's one I can't support as a representative of Martin and Channing.'

'So,' Channing said in a thin, nasal tone that served to emphasize his nervousness. 'Where do we go from here?'

'Out,' Eric replied.

'What the hell's that supposed to mean?' Everett demanded.

'It means I must insist that Channing withdraws the bank's support from the Salamander defence. And if he has gone through with the share purchase, using Martin and Channing funds—rather than promising to do so—that deal must be resiled from.'

226

'Or what?'

'Or I'll expose the whole strategy of the Salamander chill,' Eric said pleasantly.

'I'd break your back first,' Paul Everett snarled. Eric looked at him: he had always suspected there were subdued fires of violence in the man, largely damped down by his need to present an acceptable face to his business colleagues, but Eric recalled Jack Johnson's summary of him as a womanizing, egocentric tough. In the right circumstances the veneer would peel away and the real violence emerge. Perhaps the circumstances were approaching.

Leonard Channing cleared his throat. Eric could see that the banker was shaken: his patrician features seemed suddenly drawn and his mouth had lost its customary composure. There was a greyness about his skin which drew attention to his age, something one was rarely aware of because of the innate sharpness of the man. He was looking at Paul Everett and there was a hesitancy about him that was uncharacteristic. 'We'll have to talk about this.'

Hugh Nelson raised an eyebrow, still in control, sidelined and not allowing himself to be drawn into the argument too deeply. He was not averse to pushing it along, nevertheless. 'Talk about what, Channing? No secret discussion with Everett, please: if the chill is to be undermined we all need to know what's happening.'

'I . . . my board will need confirmation . . .' Channing was conscious of pressure from Eric and he didn't like it. He swallowed his pride with difficulty. 'I will need confirmation, in addition, that none of the share purchases made to date, or planned, exceed five per cent of the stock. The necessity for disclosure—'

'Dammit, Channing,' Everett interrupted, glowering at him from under heavy brows, 'don't start getting lily-livered with me now. The chill is biting; the share price is going up again; the market signs for the next month are looking good; there's every chance we can beat the hell out of Gower and Rue and then it'll just be a matter of mopping up—'

'Everything I've said still stands,' Eric intervened, watching Channing's hesitation. 'And you haven't had your confirmation, have you?'

There was a long silence. Channing looked down at the plate in front of him. Like the others, he hadn't touched it. 'I think . . . I think we need time.'

Everett began to say something, then stopped. The room was still, silent except for their breathing. In an abrupt motion Channing stood up. 'I'll have to get back to the bank. Everett, I'll call you later this afternoon. I think we'd better leave things at that point, now we have, so clearly, this ultimatum from Ward.'

'Time's running out, Channing,' Eric warned.

Channing glared at him but there was little fire in his eyes. He turned and walked out of the room. Everett rose. His mouth was grim, his eyes like slate. He bunched his fists as he looked towards Eric. 'There'll come a time . . .' he threatened.

Only Hugh Nelson seemed still at ease, but perhaps his stake in this was less than the others. He might be having his own problems outside this room with the DTI investigation rumoured into Reeves Grenham, but in the Salamander battle he was only an adviser and a strategist. Eric's intervention had threatened that strategy, but that merely meant he would now have to come up with some alternatives if Salamander was to beat off the challenge from Gower and Rue. He managed a thin smile as he appraised Eric, as though he had never really seen him before. 'Quite a performance, Ward. You've done your homework well. Clearly, you have contacts in the City.'

'Don't we all?' Eric replied, recalling a conversation he had had with Nelson concerning Morcomb Estates' intentions regarding Roger Graham, Ltd.

'Hah . . . but my guess is you've been talking to a financial journalist, maybe, or a

City analyst. No matter, it all helps us stir the pot. And who knows what the next twenty-four hours may bring? That's what you have to learn about the City—plan long, but expect short-term hiccups. I'll be seeing you, Ward.'

He smiled and walked out, a confident, arrogant young man; likeable, but cold. He had coined the word for this defence strategy and maybe it was a mechanism he always employed in his own life: always depend on your own resources to kill off the opposition. That was what the chill had been about—the salamander, freezing out the danger to itself.

Eric walked across to the window, thinking. He stood there, looking out over the park to the London streets beyond, bustling with life and noise, and he thought about Channing returning to the bank. He would be ringing Everett: he would *have* to get the confirmations, and when he didn't get them he would have no option but to pull out.

There was a tap on the door. The waiter looked in; his eyebrows rose when he saw the untouched plates. 'Can I clear away, sir?'

Eric nodded. 'We've finished.'

He walked past the waiter, glanced at his watch and turned towards the stairs. As he reached the top of the marble staircase he caught a glimpse of Chris Graham in the lobby. He was heading for the main entrance. He seemed to be in something of a hurry.

Probably running to give the Grahams what he considered to be good news, Eric thought grimly. He wondered how they'd take it.

He made his way down the staircase, his hand gently sliding along the polished banister. There were a few people lounging around in the lobby, but no one he recognized: the war cabinet had all gone.

Eric walked across to the uniformed porter behind the desk. 'I'm expecting a visit from a young lady.'

'Yes, sir?'

'Her name's Sanderson. Has she arrived, in the last few minutes?'

'I'll just check, sir.'

The porter stepped behind the partition and walked into the office beyond. An older man came out, wings of grey carefully brushed back below a bald patch on the top of his head. 'Mr Ward?'

'That's right.'

'The young lady you mention—Miss Sanderson. She arrived here about twenty minutes ago. She asked for you, and I directed her to sit in the ladies' room, the waiting-room just across the lobby over there. She'd be able to see you when you came down the stairs, then.'

Ladies' waiting-room. Some things never changed in the clubs, Eric thought, smiling to himself. He turned, began to walk across the lobby. The man with the grey hair called after

231

him.

'Mr Ward, I'm sorry, I didn't make myself clear.'

'What do you mean?'

'She arrived about twenty minutes ago, and I directed her over there, and she waited for a while. But then, suddenly, she left again.'

'*She left?*'

The man looked at him, lowering his head confidentially. 'Another appointment, I would imagine, sir.'

Eric frowned. 'I don't understand.'

'Well, sir, she left as though she realized she was late for another appointment. I mean, one moment she was there, and the next she was rushing out through the main entrance.'

'*Rushing?*'

The man smiled. 'If you don't mind me making the allusion, sir, your young lady friend went out through those doors just like a startled rabbit!'

2

Eric went up to his room, puzzled and edgy. He could not account for Freda Sanderson's behaviour, but the words used by the porter left a cold feeling in his stomach. He picked up the phone, hesitated, glanced at his watch. If she had decided to return to her flat she would hardly have reached there yet—there was no point in ringing. *If* she had gone there. It could have been the reaction of a

232

frightened woman.

Frightened. Of what?

And if she'd suddenly got scared of what she was doing, had had time to reflect, sitting there with the book, waiting for Eric, changed her mind, gone back to her flat . . . would she stay there?

Or would she move on?

Eric gritted his teeth; he couldn't lose her now, and he wanted to see that book. He made his way quickly downstairs and asked the porter in the lobby to call him a taxi.

It arrived some ten minutes later. Annoyed by the delay, largely due to traffic hold-ups the cabbie explained, Eric was short in his manner, directing him to Freda Sanderson's address. It possibly accounted for the taxi-driver's reaction: an uncharacteristic, sullen silence as they drove across London, and the suggestion that 'This should do you 'ere, guv, won't it?' when they were still on the main road some three hundred yards from the mews flat side-street. Eric noted the bowler-hatted character with his arm raised and knew that the cabbie scented a useful fare. He got out, paid the fare. It was just as easy, instead of arguing: the taxi would have had to drive to the lights at the end of the road and turn there in any case. And Eric was reluctant to incur more delay: Freda Sanderson might have flown the nest.

The traffic was heavy; he had to wait for

almost a minute to cross the road. He was suddenly filled with a sense of foreboding: time was slipping away, the girl could be on her way . . . but there was something else too, and the prickling was back in his eyes as the adrenalin began to surge in his veins.

He crossed the road and turned into the side-street which led down to the mews. Expensive cars were parked along its length; surprisingly, there were a number of free spaces in spite of the bustle in the main road. A Porsche, badly parked . . . a Mercedes, two Rovers . . . a Peugeot . . . an elegant Toyota, a young man getting into it with a girl. They were both laughing.

The building he wanted was just ahead. He approached the entrance, wondering how he could get in if she refused to answer his call when he used the phone. He stepped up to the door and realized it was not quite closed. Puzzled, he pressed the door lightly and it swung open: he was in the lobby.

He closed the door behind him; it seemed to stick a little but a little gentle pressure and it closed easily enough. Eric frowned. If Freda Sanderson had come in, hurriedly, she might have left the door to swing to behind her, not applying sufficient pressure.

On the other hand, if someone had wanted to make as little noise as possible . . .

A pulse beat in Eric's forehead and his hands were suddenly clammy. He strode across to the entrance to Freda Sanderson's flat. He rang the bell. Silence followed. He rang the bell again.

There was no answer.

But there was something wrong. Eric felt it: in the air, in the atmosphere, in the prickling of his skin. The years in the police force in Northumberland had taught him to rely upon that instinct. He stepped back, looked at the door, and its Yale lock.

He knew the technique.

Without thinking more, he raised his foot and crashed it against the door. It was flimsy; it splintered with a harsh, cracking sound. He attacked it again, the blood pounding now in his temples and the hinges gave way, the door sagging backwards: one more crash and it was ripped away from its supports and Eric staggered into the hallway of the flat.

It was dimmer than he had expected: the curtains were drawn and there were no lights on. He walked towards the sitting-room and turned, to look about him when the soft, sibilant sound behind him made him whirl, try to avoid the blow he knew was coming.

It caught him heavily, painfully, on the back of his neck, numbing his shoulder-blade, dizzying him, sending him to his knees. A second blow followed but again it was wild, striking him across the shoulder, missing his head, but its force was sufficient to send him sprawling. He lay almost spreadeagled, half-conscious, and there was a long moment when he could hear a man's harsh breathing, felt the hesitation in his attacker, a decision to be made . . .

His senses faded to the sound of his assailant moving away, back to the destroyed door, out into the hallway. Then, for a while, there was silence.

Coloured lights danced behind his eyes; he thought of Karen O'Neill, and Nick Graham's face merged with hers until they became one face; the beating of the blood in his head was insistent and demanding and he could feel the pile of the carpet under his fingers. Full consciousness was returning, but slowly; painfully, Eric raised his head and winced as the stabbing agony shot through his shoulder. He managed to roll over, began to sit up, and he saw the small case lying on the floor, its contents scattered from the burst lid.

He knew now what had happened. He rose to his feet carefully; he breathed deeply, waiting for the dizziness to stop. Then he walked across to the bedroom.

She was still fully clothed. She was lying on the floor, on her back. Her eyes were wide open, engorged, staring. Her tongue had forced its way between her teeth; it looked black and swollen.

The scarf—brightly coloured, thin silk—was still around her neck. It had cut deep, as it had strangled the life out of Freda Sanderson.

★ ★ ★

He hadn't been able to come up with many answers when the police arrived. He went along with them while an incident room was set up, the forensic people came, the photographers were called for. A doctor gave him some painkillers, and he was interrogated at the local headquarters by a not unsympathetic detective-inspector. Eric knew the routine; and he knew there was little he could tell them.

She had been coming to see him with some information which *might* have had some connection with the death of Karen O'Neill. Something had made her change her mind and she had returned to the flat, packed a case, and was getting ready to leave. The rest was largely guesswork: as she had opened the door to leave someone had pushed her back into the hallway, hit her with sufficient force to half-daze her, and then dragged her into the bedroom, where he had strangled her.

He had either opened the case and had been looking for something—possibly, the book, Eric suggested, or it had burst in the struggle.

There was little to go on. She had not managed to get her nails into the killer: it seemed there were no obvious scrapings

237

under her nails, although that would be for forensic to confirm later.

'I think you'd better see the doctor again,' the detective-inspector suggested in a kindly tone. 'You're looking a bit groggy.'

Eric shrugged. 'I don't know. At least, you can go ahead and arrange for the release of Jim Edmonds now.'

'Why is that, sir?'

'Because he's still inside. He couldn't have got out and killed Freda Sanderson.'

'But you must realize no connection has yet been demonstrated between the deaths of Karen O'Neill and Freda Sanderson.'

'Bloody hell! Are you telling me it's *coincidence* that you get two killings in the same building?' An unnatural anger seized Eric: the blood punded dizzily in his head and the back of his skull ached. He felt odd, unable to concentrate properly.

'I'll arrange for you to get into St Mark's; they'll keep you under observation tonight,' the detective-inspector was saying. 'You're still shaky . . . concussion, I expect. You were like that when we found you in the street.'

'Street?' Eric was puzzled for a few moments, not understanding. 'Oh yes. After the phone call, after I called you . . . I went out into the street.'

'Why did you do that?'

'I was dizzy . . . needed fresh air.'

No. There was something else. Behaving like a good copper, that's what he'd been doing. But he wasn't a copper, he was a solicitor now.

Checking, just checking . . .

'I'll arrange for a car, sir,' the detective-inspector said. His voice seemed a long way distant, like the voices of children playing on a sunny summer afternoon on the rolling Northumberland hills.

3

Eric spent the night in the hospital. He rang Anne and told her what had happened, underplaying the violence that had occurred so that she was not too much worried, and told her they were keeping him in for observation. There was every expectation that he would be released to come home the next day. He would fly back, as soon as he had checked on the outcome of the discussion between Paul Everett and Leonard Channing.

He slept badly that night in the hospital. It might have been the strangeness of his surroundings, but his sleep was fitful and lit with confused dreams in which people and places and events tumbled one over the other in a disturbing mélange that left him tossing and turning in a seemingly airless room.

The police came again the next morning to take a statement from him, and to check whether there was anything more he could add: there was not, though even as he said it, something niggled at the back of his mind. Again he was asked if he could provide a description of his attacker; once again he said he could not. He had been attacked from behind, and had seen nothing in the dim, curtained room. All he could confirm was that the assailant had been a man.

At the end of the interview the detective-inspector agreed there was no reason why he should not be allowed to return home to Northumberland. The doctor, when he arrived later that morning, was less confident.

'I'd prefer if you stayed in another day,' he suggested, fingers straying to his lapel. 'You're still concussed; you need rest; and I'd really like to have Mr Farley look at you. He's an eye specialist . . . I mean, we don't want anything to have gone wrong in that direction, do we, with your history . . .'

Eric was forced to accept the judgment; he was still feeling dizzy, and although his vision did not seem to have been affected, the proposal the doctor was making seemed sensible. Anne approved of it, when he told her over the phone, but he refused to allow her to come down to London to collect him. It was not necessary, he assured her.

Nor was it, he felt next morning. He felt fine. His vision was as normal, he ached along the shoulder and there was a faint ringing still in his ears on occasions, but it was ridiculous staying in hospital any longer. He felt fit enough to leave. He discharged himself.

There was a moment in the street, as he left the taxi outside his club, when a wave of dizziness came back but it passed almost at once. He collected his things from the room still booked for him at the club, then picked up the phone, calling the office of Leonard Channing.

Channing's secretary answered.

'I'm afraid Mr Channing can't be disturbed, Mr Ward.'

She had a way of pronouncing his name that irritated him; the inflection was tinged with contempt.

'It's urgent I talk to him.'

'I regret—'

'Never mind regretting. Get him on the phone.' Eric was determined not to be fobbed off: he wanted to know what Channing had agreed with Everett.

'Mr Ward, I'm *sorry*,' the secretary insisted frigidly. 'Mr Channing is in a meeting and expressly said—'

'Who's he with?'

'I beg your . . . I'm sorry, Mr Ward, I don't think I can let you—'

'*Listen*. I know it's a very important position you hold. But I *am* a director of Martin and Channing. I want to know what the meeting is that he's attending. The board?'

Flustered, she said, 'No, it's not exactly a meeting of Martin and Channing—'

'Is Paul Everett with him?'

'Mr Everett is there, yes, and—'

'That'll do.' Eric put down the phone. He could imagine her sitting there, flurried, her agate eyes annoyed behind her spectacles, her middle-aged features flushed. She'd not be someone he could ever ask a favour of. His head was aching slightly, a vague, indeterminate pain.

Why had he gone out into the street after finding Freda Sanderson?

He rang down to the lobby and asked the porter to call him a cab.

*   *   *

Leonard Channing didn't like it. His thin nostrils were dilated with anger; his eyes were slitted and the edges of his mouth were hard with disapproval as he stared at Eric. The stiff-backed secretary was standing behind Eric, ready to close the door. Channing wanted to make the point in front of her, but thought better of it: Eric was a member of the board of the merchant bank. His glance slipped past to her and he nodded. With her nose in the air she left the room, closing the door with an excessive quietness.

'You weren't invited to this meeting,

242

Ward.'

'I wasn't even told about it.'

'Are you sure you're fit? We heard about—'

'I'm fit.' Eric sat down, and looked around. Apart from Channing, there were three other men facing him: Paul Everett, Hugh Nelson, and a man he had never seen before.

Channing tried again. 'This meeting is an exploratory one—'

'About Salamander?'

'That's so, but—'

'Then I'd better be here,' Eric said flatly.

Channing spoke with an effort, restraining himself. 'It's not a meeting precisely about . . . about the discussion we had and I'm not sure—'

'If it's about Salamander, I need to be here,' Eric insisted. There was a buzzing in his ears now and he felt his temper rising, irrationally.

Channing breathed through his thin nostrils; it came out as an impatient sigh. 'Well, if you're sure you're fit enough. Mr Pearson, this is one of my colleagues on the board of Martin and Channing . . . Mr Ward. He was involved in some unpleasantness a couple of days ago.'

From the venomous glance Channing directed to Eric it was clear he felt the unpleasantness could have been greater.

'Mr Pearson,' Channing added, 'is an inspector employed in the Department of

Trade and Industry.'

He was small-boned, bespectacled, with thinning reddish hair and a mouth that found it easy to smile. The smile was an artificial aid, however, a prop for conversation, something that could be switched on and off from time to time to emphasize a point. His eyes were sharp and intelligent: he wore a grey, pin-striped suit like a uniform and when he rose to shake hands with Eric his grip was surprisingly strong, testing in its firmness. He would be a man accustomed to evasion and used to ignoring it. From the tension in the room it was clear that he had already met some, sidestepped it, and was pursuing the line of inquiry.

'I was just saying,' Pearson announced to Eric, 'that the conversation we're having here is just exploratory, and off the record. There's nothing *formal* about my request for an interview with the group; it was simply that I felt a meeting might help clear the air, establish a few points of principle; maybe get rid of some misconceptions that seem to be flying around.' The smile came on like a red light and vanished again. 'From your side as well as ours, of course.'

Eric was interested. He had come in to find out the result of the Everett-Channing conversation, but he seemed to have stepped into a different nest of hornets. This request from the DTI might be exploratory, but it was also a thunderous warning shot across the bows of Salamander, and everyone in the room knew it.

'What I'd particularly like to explore with you,' Pearson was saying in a friendly, offhand manner, 'are the events leading up to the counter-offer that Salamander made in response to the Gower and Rue bid that we approved. If one of you could take me through . . . ?'

He glanced around. Sourly, Paul Everett hunched himself forward in his seat and nodded. 'I suppose it would be best if *I* took you through them . . .'

Everett's voice took on a droning note, as though he was reciting a well-worn text. Pearson was listening carefully and smiling a faint-edged smile; Nelson was inspecting his nails; Leonard Channing was flicking nervously through some papers in front of him, as though expecting to be called upon any minute now and eager to prepare himself for the ordeal.

Eric found his attention wandering. He was listening to Everett, but as he watched him he began to think about his visit to Garden City Enterprises. What was it Johnson had told him about Everett? A womanizer; a man who had married three times yet still had affairs; a man who might possibly have come across Karen O'Neill. One of a breed: City men who could not switch off after the heady excitement of a day spent trading in millions and needed to keep burning the candle. Eric's glance slipped to Hugh Nelson. Was the arbitrageur one of those men?

He wished he could remember precisely why he had gone out into the street after finding the body of Freda Sanderson.

'Perhaps now,' Pearson was saying, 'you'd care to explain to me in some detail the nature of your defence strategy. I'm aware you'll wish to keep back some information, of course—' the smile broadened, friendly, understanding, then vanished again—'but if you could perhaps sketch it out for me. I remind you, there's nothing formal in this visit. Just an exploration . . .'

There was a new tension in the room now; Channing's eyes slipped involuntarily towards Eric. Clearly he was nervous, worried that Eric might intervene at the wrong time, divulge something of their recent arguments to the detriment of the Salamander situation. Eric had no such intention: it was not his place to destroy Salamander; merely to protect the bank. He sat and he listened as Everett went over the ground carefully, talking about the fan club but omitting the re-purchase guarantees and the methods of persuasion. As he spoke, gradually, the buzzing in Eric's head eased and he began to feel more normal. By the time the coffee came his head felt clear, and he could think straight.

And at last he remembered why he had gone back into the street after Freda Sanderson died.

*   *   *

The morning drew to a close. Pearson had questioned Everett closely, but had made little comment about Channing's presentation, when he discussed the financial package the merchant bank had put together for Salamander. He expressed himself satisfied, but Eric had no doubt that the inspector had not been fooled by Everett's performance: this would not be the last they would hear from the DTI.

Pearson leaned back in his chair. 'Well, gentlemen, I think it's necessary for me to thank you for your patience this morning. I'm a lot clearer now about the position and—'

'You'll be investigating the Reeves Grenham issue as well, I imagine,' Eric said suddenly.

Momentarily, Pearson was taken aback. 'Er . . . well, yes, I'm involved with some colleagues in looking at the matter of insider dealing in that affair. But—'

'We were a bit concerned at one point,' Eric went on cheerfully. 'You know, having an arbitrageur advising on the Salamander defence might have rebounded on us.'

Hugh Nelson had turned his head. His eyes were icy as he glared at Eric. Pearson was slightly embarrassed. 'No, we don't work that way. The . . . the fact that Mr Nelson is involved here has no bearing—'

'Channing mentioned I'd been involved in some *unpleasantness*. Had you heard about it?'

'No, I—'

'It was a matter of murder.'

The room was silent. All four men stared at Eric as though he had introduced a forbidden topic into the discussion.

'I'm afraid—'

Eric cut across Pearson again. 'It has City connections, so I thought it might be useful to pick up any vibrations you've sensed in the matter.'

Pearson was breathing lightly, a nervous smile at the edge of his mouth. He was a perceptive man, one used to evasions and nuances, and Eric knew he was suddenly aware of the new tensions in the room. It interested him. He raised an interrogative eyebrow. 'I can't say I've picked up any information . . . *City* connections, you say?'

'Well, in the sense that there's a story going the rounds that the victim was a City-available whore; you know, available to hyped-up businessmen who couldn't sleep at night.'

'Is that so?'

'It's a story. I don't believe it myself,' Eric

said.

'Who exactly are we talking about?' Channing intervened.

'Oh, Karen O'Neill, of course,' Eric said brightly.

Everett frowned, leaning forward. 'But this thing *you* were involved with the other day—'

'The murder of Freda Sanderson. Oh yes. It's all part of the same series of events,' Eric said.

'The murders are linked.'

'Yes.' Eric paused, watching Paul Everett carefully. 'Do you know a man called Chris Graham?'

Everett's face was smooth. He shook his head.

'What about you, Nelson? You ever come across him?'

Hugh Nelson stuck out his lower lip in thught. 'Chris Graham. Can't say I have. Is he something to do with the murders?'

'My wife's company is considering the acquisition of Roger Graham, Ltd. Chris Graham has been trying to find another buyer, recently. I just wondered whether any of you would have come across him in his travels.' Eric paused. 'He's also an old friend of Karen O'Neill's.'

Everett shook his head. 'The City's rarely interested in the kind of acquisition you're talking about. Small beer. North of Watford as well, hey? No interest. So there's little likelihood we'd meet him.'

'He was in the club the other day, when we met,' Eric said. 'The day Freda Sanderson died.'

The comment quietened them; a shadow passing over the room. Pearson frowned, caressed his lower lip with one finger. 'What's the link-up in all this, Mr Ward? And forgive me, but what's it got to do with this meeting?'

'The connection with this meeting is coincidental. It's just that, with the exception of yourself, Mr Pearson, we were *all* at the club that afternoon . . . and so was Chris Graham.'

'And—?'

'Freda Sanderson came to the club to see me. She was bringing some information with her. She reached the club, sat waiting for me—and then she saw someone she recognized in the club. It panicked her, she ran out, got a taxi back to her flat, started to pack—and then she was killed.'

'Why?'

Eric paused. 'In my view, because the person she recognized was the one she could identify as having been the lover of Karen O'Neill.'

The silence grew around them. Brows knitted, Paul Everett leaned forward. 'Is that the information she was bringing you?'

Eric shook his head. 'No. She didn't know the man's name. You see, Karen never told her the name and she deliberately didn't ask. She didn't want to get involved. She knew Karen was a tough young woman out to make the best for herself. That involved taking a lover, being kept by him in some luxury at the flat. But she was also a woman who was on the lookout for the main chance. And it seems she came across something—some information—which was valuable. Extremely valuable. But then something happened. Maybe the lover was cooling. Maybe he suspected she'd been prying into his affairs. Whatever the reason, Karen thought she would be well advised for the moment to have the information out of her possession. So she gave it to Freda Sanderson. She said it was her *insurance policy*.'

'And this was the information she was bringing to you, this Sanderson woman?' Hugh Nelson asked.

Eric nodded. 'That's right. But she saw Karen's lover in the club. *And he saw her*. When she hurried out, I guess he realized she could link him with Karen, even though she didn't know his name. He went after her. He killed her, to silence her. I arrived and he attacked me.'

'But what was the information she was carrying?' Leonard Channing asked in a nervous voice.

'I'm not sure. It was a book. It contained dates, numbers and a few names.' Eric

251

glanced at Pearson. 'I wondered whether Mr Pearson might have some thoughts on the matter.'

'Me? No . . . I can't see . . .' The smile suddenly came and switched off again as the inspector was struck by a thought. 'Unless . . .'

He was silent, thinking, watching Eric's face. 'That's why I wonder about the City connection,' Eric said softly. 'Let me hypothesize. This man is active in the City. He takes a mistress—Karen O'Neill. She becomes aware of some of his activity which borders on the . . . unethical. She's no fool. She takes notes: the dates of a few phone calls, a few names she's picked up, and possibly some numbers of bank accounts. Explosive information, in the wrong hands. They could send a man to jail.'

Pearson's eyes widened. He was getting the picture.

'When the man in question becomes suspicious—maybe he caught her listening to a call he's made—he decides she has to be removed. He does it coldly, and efficiently. That's the kind of man he is. Indeed, it's the way he always works. An attitude of mind, if you like: he summed it up in a defence strategy, when he said you should try to put out the fires that threaten you by using your own resources. Use the chill to remove the problem—the Salamander chill.'

Paul Everett began to say something angrily, but then stopped, frowning. 'But I didn't—'

'No. *You* didn't devise the strategy,' Eric said. 'Hugh Nelson did.'

Channing's head came up, a wolf scenting blood. He looked at Eric in surprise and then turned towards Nelson. The arbitrageur was at ease, lolling in his chair, confident. 'That's right. The phrase was mine. But so what?'

'As I said . . . nothing but an attitude of mind. But there are a few more things.'

'Yes?'

'How did you know about the Roger Graham acquisition plan?'

Nelson raised his eyebrows. '*I* knew about it?'

'You did,' Eric affirmed. 'You asked me about it, the first time we met. You've already told us you didn't know Chris Graham. He hadn't *started* his search for another bidder at that stage. There could have been no City gossip about the acquisition, even if, as Everett says, the City would have been so out of character as to be interested. So—how did you know about it?'

'Gossip—'

'No. I don't think so. The thing was under wraps in the North. But there was one person who could have told you. A person who came to a party at Perastino's in Newcastle. Someone who was very close to the man

253

advising Morcomb Estates. Karen O'Neill.'

Hugh Nelson raised his eyebrows, smiling thinly. 'Are you suggesting—'

'There are a few other things that sort of click into place for me now, too. Something a financial journalist told me recently. Secrets in the City, he said, are never secrets. There are always avenues for information . . . pieces of paper, names, dates . . . It was a word you used yourself, Nelson.'

'When?'

'With Everett. When he demanded to know if there was any evidence of your involvement in Reeves Grenham insider dealing.'

Pearson, the DTI inspector, leaned forward with interest. 'What was the reply, Mr Ward?'

Ward still watched Hugh Nelson. 'Everett actually asked about *loopholes*. He asked Nelson if they'd been closed. Nelson replied *all avenues have been closed*. And Everett persisted.'

'Yes?' Pearson wetted eager lips.

'*Dead?* he asked,' Eric replied. 'And Nelson confirmed it. I think now he was able to say that because Karen O'Neill was just that. *Dead.*'

Nelson grinned boyishly, shaking his head. 'You're playing with words, Ward, making suppositions and arguments out of thin air, out of innocent conversations.'

'I don't think so,' Eric disagreed. 'You chose your words with care. When you spoke to me of the Morcomb takeover of Graham's you laughed at my surprise, told me there were *always sources of information*. In this case, the information was of no use to you, so you tossed it away, being clever, trying to impress me. But I think you got that information from Karen O'Neill—and maybe when you learned the shoe was on the other foot, and *she* had got information about *you*—'

Leonard Channing cleared his throat nervously. 'You're not telling us Nelson kept this woman—'

'What car do you drive, Nelson?'

'Is that an issue?'

'When I went to Sanderson's flat,' Eric replied, 'there were several cars parked in the street. I noted them; an old policeman's instinct. After I was attacked the same instinct took me back into the street. I needed to check, find out if a car had been moved. Because the killer who hurried from the club after Freda Sanderson would probably have driven his own car—too hurried to take precautions. He'd have parked nearby to make a quick escape. When I came out of her flat, one of the cars *had* gone. It was a Porsche. What car do you drive, Nelson?'

'I don't see—'

'*A Porsche,*' Paul Everett rasped harshly.

There was a short silence. Hugh Nelson looked down at his hands; they were trembling slightly, fingers curled. His smile was stiff. 'You did say, Ward, that this was merely a hypothesis.'

'But one that should now be tested,' Eric said softly, 'by the police.'

4

'The odd thing is,' Eric said to Anne as they walked along the track to the crags, 'I don't believe Nelson ever actually knew about the book, Karen O'Neill's "insurance policy". What we're getting from the police is the suggestion that he killed her because he knew she was prepared to use information she'd acquired to blackmail him.'

'But why would she blackmail him when he had set her up in the flat?' Anne asked.

'He'd tired of her, it seems. Wanted rid of her. She then made it clear she would want a payoff: he wasn't prepared to have that hanging over him, not with the insider dealing investigation going on.'

'That's what the information was about?'

'That's right. Nelson had traded illegally in the Reeves Grenham issue and was about to be investigated by the DTI. He couldn't afford to have O'Neill around, talking about what she knew. The notebook included details of some of the dealings—they've found it in the Sanderson flat. I don't know whether

Nelson would have looked for it and found it, but my arrival prevented that. My guess is, nevertheless, he didn't even know about it: he killed Sanderson to stop her identifying him as Karen's lover—particularly when the police had as good as convinced themselves Edmonds had done the killing, in a jealous rage.'

'So she wasn't a whore after all,' Anne mused.

'Terminology.' Eric smiled. 'A kept woman, a hard woman, one whose greediness killed her. Anyway, talking of greed: what's the position on Chris Graham?'

Anne chuckled. 'They gave him a flea in the ear. It's odd, you know: when the acquisitions bid started, Roger Graham was against dealing with a woman. Now, when his youngest son hasn't played fair, has broken our agreement and attempted to sound out another buyer, some innate *chivalry* is one of the reasons why Roger Graham is so mad.'

'That old warrior? I don't believe it.'

'Well, there's self-interest too,' Anne admitted. 'He wants to see the firm continue, not get wiped out. Anyway, the upshot is, oddly enough, that they want to go ahead and are even prepared to agree a performance-related purchase—a sort of reaction to Chris Graham's foolishness. Anything he raises now gets shot down.'

'Will you use Jim Edmonds in the
257

remaining negotiations?'

Anne hesitated. 'If he's up to it. I'll ask him . . . he's had a rough time of it, and it's not over for him yet, but maybe to be drawn back in is the fillip he needs to get back on the rails again.' She smiled. 'It's not that we're a recuperative agency—he's a good man, and he knows the acquisitions business. I think it makes sense to use him.'

'So do I.'

They had reached the top of the hill. To the west the sun was low in the sky and the moorland about them was purple-blue in the fading light. A family of plover called plaintively on the hill and under Cheviot there was a glint of gold, a tint of rose on the slopes.

Eric slipped his arm lightly across Anne's shoulders. It was good to be back in the North for a few days. It would give him the chance to gear himself mentally for the board meeting at Martin and Channing. He was not yet certain how far he would push things: after his warning, Channing had not completed the deal with Everett and so the bank had suffered no financial loss. Nevertheless, the question was whether Eric should try to censure Channing for the way he had behaved. At this stage, it would probably be unwise: Eric would not have sufficient support on the board, when Leonard Channing could show no harm had occurred.

'And what about the Salamander chill?' Anne asked.

Eric shrugged. 'You saw the papers this morning. The City . . . well, you know how it is. Nelson was involved in the Salamander defence; his arrest has had repercussions. Share prices have slipped and the fan club will get even more nervous. Ranks are breaking and I don't think the DTI will need to investigate: Gower and Rue will win. It was always a gamble, the Salamander chill—it depended too much upon luck, and was based upon an illegal premise. Doesn't pay, you know, to bend the law.'

Anne laughed at the mock-seriousness of his tone. 'And there,' she said, 'there speaks a lawyer!'

Photoset, printed and bound in Great Britain by REDWOOD BURN LIMITED, Trowbridge, Wiltshire